I would like to devote this book to God because without him this would not be possible.

To my amazing husband, Depodray, who said, "Baby whatever you need, if it's in my power, I will make sure you have it. I'll be by your side every step of the way. Pour your heart out in your book, it will all pay off in the end." I love you with all my heart. I can always count on you to push me beyond my limits. Thanks babe." To my amazing princes, KeShawn, Dezmond, and Josiah, whom made this journey well worth it, and to my parents and four brothers, who motivated me to be the woman I am today.

To all my acquaintances, family, and those I met along the way who encouraged me to continue pushing forward saying, "There's somebody out there waiting to read your book including me."

To Ironworker's Wives across the globe, you are the weld that holds the metal together and the hornets that support all the weight. Without you, your husband wouldn't be able to make it through his sometimes stressful day at work. There are many great wives in the world, but we are an entirely different breed. When you first marry an Ironworker, it's like we are metal that has been placed into the fire. We are then molded to be strong when he is weak, a motivator when he wants to quit, a chiropractor when his body is out of whack, his personal alarm clock for those early mornings and late nights, his traveling agent with a built-in Gps system when he has to travel across the world to work helping build America. We have faith that he is going to be ok as he works 100 feet in the air and underground. Once we have been molded we are unbreakable. Until you have been molded to be with an Ironworker, you have no idea what it's like to be married to one.

ACKNOWLEDGMENTS

Exceptional thanks to my spiritual parents Bishop Alton Davis Jr. And pastor, first lady Michelle Davis along with True Redemption Center (TRC) family for all your support.

Extraordinary thanks to Femee hair doctor Culberson, hairstyles at mahogany Xperience hair & barber salon for doing my hair for the photo shoot. I truly loved it.

Distinctive thanks to Natalie Woodward, makeup artist/hair stylist at mahogany Xperience hair & barber salon for doing an awesome job on my makeup for the photo shoot.

Special thanks to Wendy Ainsworth, photography at graceful hope photography for capturing my vision through a small lens that produced a master piece. My pictures are marvelous.

Special thanks to Jray Crawford, graphic designs at kids play creations for making an incredible book cover.

Special thanks to pastor Stan Jones and first lady Miriam Jones along with Jerusalem Temple members(JT) for all your support.

A couple of years ago something happen, causing me to put this book away. I refuse to pick it up. Then you came along and helped me, reassuring me that we can make this book happen. I couldn't thank you enough for being there for me. Thank you so much Jazmine Lampley. You are the best editor a writer could have.

AUTHOR INTRODUCTION

While you prepare to indulge in a roller coaster ride of emotions by reading this book, I pray that you can take something from it that can help you and equip you to help someone else. Life is full of obstacles; some may be easier to overcome than others. The good thing is that there is not an obstacle that hasn't been conquered. There's nothing wrong with learning from other's past failures and successes.

WHEN YOU MARRY SOMEONE, IT'S LIKE GOING INTO A CAR DEALERSHIP TO PURCHASE A CAR. YOU'VE FOUND THE PERFECT CAR FOR YOU. THE ONE THAT WORKS BEST FOR YOU. YOU CAN'T TAKE YOUR EYES OFF OF IT AND EVERYBODY WANTS IT, BUT YOU WERE BLESSED TO SECURE IT. IT WILL HELP TAKE YOU THROUGH THE BIPOLAR WEATHER, RAIN, SLEET, SNOW, AND SUNSHINE. IT MAY HAVE HAD PREVIOUS OWNERS, BUT IT'S LIKE BRAND NEW TO YOU. AFTER YOU TOOK IT FOR A TEST DRIVE, THERE WAS NO DOUBT IN YOUR MIND THAT THIS IS THE ONE. THE DEALER INFORMS YOU THAT THE CAR IS SOLD AS IS, AND YOU'RE ALL RIGHT WITH THAT BECAUSE YOU DON'T HAVE ANY REGRETS AND NO INTENTION OF RETURNING IT. AS A RESULT, YOU SIGN THE PAPERS TO PURCHASE THE CAR. YOU DRIVE OFF THE LOT ONLY TO FIND OUT THAT DURING THE WINTER THE HEAT DOESN'T WORK PROPERLY.

NOTE: BEFORE YOU PURCHASE A CAR, BRING A MECHANIC.

PROLOGUE

Lying on the bed they once had shared was a sweet-scented pink sheet of flower border paper with the monogram "SH" in the bottom right-hand corner. The sheet was neatly folded and the top side of one fold was addressed to, "The love of my life."

Dear Max,

My love for you is endless and unconditional. My life without you is like life without fresh air or a dark tunnel without an outlet. I have never had the pleasure of meeting someone like you and couldn't have imagined marrying anyone else. You're the father of my children, my knight in shining armor, my remedy for my internal shame, and my shield from the world of pain.

While reading this letter you will soon know why I have been keeping my distance. I love you with all my heart; even more when we are apart. For that reason, I have to tell you, I'm having an affair. Sadly, it has gone on for quite some time now. I would like to insure you that I regret doing so, but I would be lying. I know you are wondering whom it is. I hate to say this but, I think you may know the guy. In fact, you two are very close, so I'm not going to give his name, I don't want to start any conflict. Besides that, I think I love him. I've tried to convince myself that it was not true. I even talk to God about it. I'm telling you this because you deserve to know. I want to stop seeing him, but I have become physically impaired, and I'm too emotionally attached. I have to admit: the physical attraction I have towards him is like nothing I've encountered. It started about two months ago while you were out of town working. I found myself crying to sleep often as any real woman would if put in my situation. Feeling desperate and neglected, I called him over. He seemed so overwhelmed when I called. This washed away any doubts that I may have had that me calling him was not the right thing to do. He did not hesitate to come over. We watched movies and talked for hours. We mainly talked about our likes and dislikes. We mentioned our dreams. Our must haves before we die. We discovered that the places we wanted to visit were very similar. We talked about all the famous people we would like to meet. The number of kids we would like to have and their genders. The affair began after that night. He always made himself available when I could not talk to you about the way I was feeling or how my day went. He sent flowers to my job even though I never required him to do so. He made me feel wonderful, placing me on a high pedestal; regardless how hard the ground shook I was not coming down. He always went out of his way to please me. He knew what I had a need of before I realized I had need of it, how cute was that? This went on for weeks. I did not believe we would ever jump to the next level, since we were just hanging out from time to time, nothing dangerous. I hoped you would keep your promise about coming home after working on the job for a month. Instead, you stayed out of town because the job had an optional four-day shut in. You tried convincing me that we needed the money, highlighting my desires and reminding me of things I couldn't afford to pay. You said you staying was the only way. We both could attest to that being a lie. You had been in that location for over three weeks working seven days a week, twelve-hour shifts, making twenty-eight dollars, and fifty cents an hour. We had no problem paying our bills on time. I felt you just put money before me. Ironically, after getting off the phone with you, he called asking could he come over. He purchased the new Underworld movie and insisted I watch it with him. Down and lonely, I said yes. He came over, and we watched the movie. While watching the movie, I put my head down, to hide my shame and began to cry. He wrapped his arms around me and wiped my tears with the tip of his sleeve. My heart raced as I sat back; taking a quick glance of his arresting lips. That moment I knew if I did not kiss him I would never know what it feels like to be with a man that did not mind giving me the world, even but for a moment. So I did just that. We kissed, and it went downhill from there; or should I say up? I mentioned before, the chemistry was like no other. Incautiously, I allowed him to stay the night. After a night like that he earned at least a night's stay with breakfast in bed with a large cup of freshly squeezed orange juice. Although I enjoyed him, I knew I couldn't hold on to the both of you, so I made my decision. I no longer want to be with you, the person you have become. Truth is the man I'm having an affair with, I only see in my dreams. He's a man who needs no introduction. He's rather tall and ridiculously handsome. He has smooth, flawless caramel skin. His eyes are big, brown, and soulful. His lips are full and assembled with perfection. He has pretty white teeth with an irresistible smile that would drive any woman wild, and a deep voice that will make you melt internally right where you stand. He maintains a low haircut. His arm muscles have muscles and he carries a six pack well. He dresses as if he has six figures in the bank. He sports the latest styles enhancing his ultimate sex appeal. Many won't mind attesting to him having a personal drive to do his best at everything. Therefore, he masters everything he touches. No Exceptions. I said I wasn't going to give a name, but for your sake I will. The man I've been having an affair with is Max James Houston, the man I first fell in love with. He loved me unconditionally and would give me the world if he knew I wanted it, with or without a price tag. I want a divorce from the man that puts money before me, who neglects me and who feels that I'm ok as long as I never have to want for anything."

Sincerely,

Sarah

Sarah placed the pink note on the bed over ten times, five different ways in hopes to make it perfectly visible so Max could see it when he got home from work. She questioned herself. Was this even necessary? Has our relationship gone that far off the deep end? Well, I did mean everything I wrote. It wasn't like it's not true, she recalled. "This letter can either bring us closer together or push us further apart. Am I really ready for that?" She sighed, taking a deep, mysterious breath. Feeling heartbroken and replaceable, she laid down on the bedroom floor, staring at the rotating ceiling fan, rationalizing her thoughts while the soft music triggered her emotions. She became sick as she recapped.

"When did our relationship diminish to this?

CHAPTER ONE

On the night two great college football teams played, Kansas City vs Kansas, Max sat in his truck in a fast food parking lot staring at a green four-door Suzuki SUV that pulled up beside him. Sarah parked in the restaurant parking lot and turned her car off. She looked in the mirror as she applied lip gloss to her lips. She noticed a man staring at her. She wasn't surprised that he was staring. She got a lot of stares most times. Eyes fixed on her left her irritated and bothered, so she did what she did often to many people and ignored him. She got out of the SUV and walked toward the door of the packed fast food restaurant located near Central West End in St. Louis, Missouri.

"Hey!" Max yelled to Sarah. He was sitting in his truck with the door open.

Sarah rolled her eyes before turning around. "Huh," She mumbled.

"Hey? How are you?" asked Max walking up to Sarah.

"You're not going to buy my food," Sarah replied bluntly before walking into the restaurant.

Max's stomach sank as her words triggered his pride. He stood outside the door looking at Sarah. He ran back to his truck, grabbed his keys out of the ignition and slammed the truck door before dashing toward the restaurant. He walked into the restaurant and began looking for Sarah. He remembered her beautiful light skin tone and long curly hair gathered into a ponytail. He walked around many hungry football fans who were hoping to make it home in time to watch the game before it started. Max smiled when he spotted Sarah. He moved close to her not saying anything. Her presence alone gave him chills.

"That'll be $13.65," said the cashier.

Sarah dug in her purse looking for her debit card.

"Here you go, ma'am." Said Max handing the cashier a

twenty-dollar bill. He put his wallet back into his back pocket.

"Here's your change, sir." The cashier held her hand out.

"You keep it," Max replied looking down at Sarah.

Sarah looked up at Max and smiled, refusing to blush. She was curious to know Max motive behind paying for her food. Like many men she's encountered, she was sure he had one, and it wasn't a good one. "Thank you."

"The pleasure is all mine." Max smiled.

They moved to the side to wait for Sarah's food.

"I'm Max. What's your name?" Max extended his hand.

Sarah looked up at him. *Should I tell him my name? He may be another Kenny, and I don't have time for that or another bozo. He did buy my food, though.*

"Sarah." She relentlessly shook his hand.

"Would you like to sit down? I know it's going to be a while before your food is ready."

"Sure." Sarah looked around for a place to sit. She spotted an empty table in the corner by the window and sat down.

"You are so…"

"Don't," said Sarah, cutting Max off.

"I get tired of hearing that. Sometimes I think my looks are a curse rather than a blessing."

Max swallowed as he tried not to stare at Sarah beautiful brown eyes and small glossy lips.

"Oh, I'm sorry." Max looked out into the crowd.

"This is ridiculous, all these football fans." Sarah glanced at the fans wearing football jerseys, hats, and slightly painted faces.

"I take it you don't like football."

"I've never sat down and tried to understand it. Looks like a bunch of men chasing each other."

Max laughed.

"Where are you from? You talk country as that one thang." Sarah stared at Max as he licked his nicely proportioned lips.

"Well, I'm from down south."

"What brings you here?"

Sarah's receipt number popped on the screen. "That's my

number." She pushed back from the table.

"Wait!" Max put his hand over Sarah's.

Sarah's heart pounded as she snatched her hand back.

"I'm sorry. I didn't mean any harm. I was trying to say that I'll go get your food for you so that you wouldn't have to push through the crowd."

"Oh, thanks. I'll get it."

Sarah walked to get her food. She checked her bag to make sure her order was correct, then started walking toward the exit.

"Yeah, baby!" A man yelled as he walked alongside Sarah. "Let's go Kansas!"

Sarah jumped. She stared at the heavy man with paint on his face.

"I'm sorry." the man said, moving quickly away from Sarah.

She turned her head and saw Max looking at her. She took a deep breath and walked towards him. Max smirked.

"Hey, do you have somewhere you have to be?" Sarah asked.

"Not really." Max hesitated.

"Do you want to sit down with me and finish talking?"

Max smiled. "Yeah, let me go get my food."

Sarah waited at the table while Max went back to his truck. *Now why did I ask him to sit with me? I hope he's not weird like Kenny.* Sarah wanted to focus on getting her life on track because she was tired of being derailed. She promised herself she wouldn't get involved with anyone.

"I'm back." said Max, sitting down across from Sarah.

"Ugh, isn't your food cold?" Sarah frowned.

"No, well a little."

"So what brought you here to St. Louis?" Sarah asked, sipping her juice.

"I'm just passing through. I'm on my way to Alaska."

"Alaska! The state where it's cold?"

"Yes."

"What black person you know want to go where it's cold?"

Max laughed.

"What are you going to do there?"

"Work."

"What kind of work? You're a fisherman?" She chuckled.

"No. I'm a Journeyman Ironworker." He smiled.

"Never heard of it. What do you do exactly?"

"I travel to different states to work. We build multi-story buildings, stadiums, arenas, hospitals, towers, bridges just to name a few."

"Wow. I've always wanted to travel. See places outside of Saint Louis. I've been to a couple of places…." Sarah's voice trailed. "I thought construction workers build most of the buildings you named. Honestly, I never thought about who would be crazy enough to build a tall bridge over all that water."

He chuckled. "A lot of people do; not many people know about Ironworkers."

"So let's cut to the chase. Where is your wife? Girlfriend? The friend with benefits?"

"I don't have any of those." He sounded convincing.

Sarah tilted her head in disbelief. It seemed everyone she talked to end up having someone else.

"It's hard to believe you don't have anyone. You cute, you in shape, you got a good job.. I'm not buying it.

Sarah's phone rang. She held up her finger before answering her phone. "Hey…. Yeah, I'm still coming." She looked up at Max and stared into his brown almond shaped eyes. "Ok. I'm headed your way now." She hung up her phone.

"I am supposed to meet up with a friend. He just called and said he's been waiting for me for the past twenty minutes." She grabbed a pen out of her purse. She picked up a napkin and wrote her number on it and slid it across the table.

"Call me sometime."

CHAPTER TWO

Max and Sarah talked over the phone every day and spent time together when they weren't busy with work. Two months into the four months of their evolving relationship, Max showed Sarah that he wanted more for the both of them, but Sarah didn't budge on her decision to keep Max in the friend zone. While at home one afternoon, Sarah was looking over some property listings in hopes to find her dream home. She looked down on her phone as it vibrated on the bed.

She smiled and picked up her phone.

"Hello." answered Sarah.

"Hey, how are you?" asked Max.

"I'm great and you?"

"I'm good. I was thinking about you and decided to give you a call."

Sarah's phone beeped. "Hold on a second."

Sarah clicked over to the other caller.

"What took you so long to answer? Must be caking," said Lauren.

Lauren was Sarah's best friend. They had been friends since middle school.

"Shut up. I'm on the phone with Max."

"Girl tell him you gone call him back; I have something to tell you."

"No. He just called. He's probably at work, so I'll call you back."

"Bye!" Lauren yelled.

Sarah switched back over to Max.

"Hey, I'm sorry. That was Lauren."

"It's cool. I'll call you later. My lunch break is over. I have to get back to work."

"Ok."

Sarah got off the phone with Max and called Lauren back.

"It took you long enough." said Lauren.

"What's up? What did you have to tell me?"

"Nothing. I was trying to see if you would get off the phone with Max."

"You're such a hater."

"So what's going on with you and him?"

"Nothing. We are just cool." Sarah sat up in the bed.

"I think he wants more." Lauren suggested. "Why won't you give him a chance? He seems like a pretty good guy compared to the other scumbags you've talked to."

"I know, but something is not right about him."

"What? You think he's gay?"

"Girl no. Shut up!" They both laughed. "He's too perfect. He has a good job making almost six figures. He's sexy as I don't know what. Doesn't have multiple baby mommas. Man, I promise it's too good to be true. You know how you see a dress you like, and you look at the tag and it's too expensive, so you go to put it back on the rack, and the rack say it's sixty percent off. You get excited. You try it on. Take it to the cashier to find out it was hanging on the wrong clothing rack."

"Oh yeah. I've been there."

"Well, that's how I feel about Max." Sarah got off the bed and walked into the living room. "Lauren, I don't think you understand how I feel. Hannah even likes him, and you know how protective I am about her. It took four months before I even introduced him to her, and Max kept asking to meet her."

"Yeah. Did you introduce them? I forgot."

"Girl, no. He wanted me to meet him. He said he had something for me. I couldn't find a babysitter. Him wanting to meet me was unexpected, so I brought her with me and the rest was history. Hannah always asks about Max now."

"Well, friend all I can say is play it by ear. You know the truth will come out sooner or later. I have to go to work in the morning, so I'll call you tomorrow."

As time went on, Sarah couldn't help but fall for Max. Every holiday, Max made sure he ended it at Sarah's apartment.

She had no doubt in her mind that Max wasn't everything he appeared to be. She wrote him love letters and persuaded her sister to drive fifty minutes to Max's job just so she could put the letter on Max's windshield. Sarah hadn't seen Max in a while due to his crazy work schedule, so one night, she decided to pop up over his cousin's house where he was staying.

Her breathing grew heavy and her palms became sweaty as she sat in front of his cousin's home. She swallowed hard. She drove off and headed home. She called Max but didn't get an answer.

Half way home she got a private call. She ignored it serval times before finally answering the call.

"Hello."

"Sarah?" asked the woman on the other end.

"Who is this?" Sarah said, twisting up her face.

"I'm sorry to call you so late. I was wondering if you can help me. You see, I found your number on a napkin as I was doing laundry."

Sarah shook her head.

"I later saw several calls being made to you, so I decided to call you."

"Ok, so how can I be of assistance to you?" Sarah remained calm.

"Do you know Max?"

Sarah's stomach caved in.

"Max who? What's his last name?"

"Houston."

"Yeah, he's an ironworker. What about him?"

"Did you know he had a girlfriend?"

"Get out of here." Sarah laughed. "Stop playing on my phone."

"I'm not playing. We stay together."

"Sure he does. He told me that he stayed with you." Sarah laughed once more. "Who is this? His cousin Karen?"

"No, this is not Karen. This is his girlfriend. He's right here. Hold on."

There was a brief silence.

"Max, get the phone! It's Sarah!"

Sarah heard moans.

"What? Man, why you call her?" Max yelled.

"He doesn't want to talk." the woman said slyly.

Sarah bit down on her lip to prevent herself from screaming. "I should have known."

Sarah's phone beeped. She hung up on Max's girlfriend and answered the other line.

"Sarah, I'm so sorry." Max said frantically. "I never meant to hurt you. I'm just in a rough position right now, and she's letting me stay her an..."

"It's cool."

Sarah's phone beeped. She clicked over.

"Yeah, he locked himself in the bathroom. You know I lied. I've known about you for a while now, Sarah."

Sarah listened as Max's ex-girlfriend told her why she waited so long to call her.

"Well I'm going to get off the phone now," Sarah said as her phone beeped.

They got off the phone. Sarah answered her other line. She listened to Max beg her to understand. He told her he was sorry once more and that he understood if she didn't want to see him anymore. Sarah got off the phone feeling betrayed; however, she didn't allow Max nor his girlfriend to tear her apart mentally or emotionally. As time moved on, so did Sarah— at least she did the best she could. She continued to work and take care of Hannah before this chaos hit her life. Max called Sarah every day and so did Max's girlfriend. She left messages on Sarah's voicemail telling her how much she hated Sarah for messing around with Max. She told Sarah that because of her, Max and her relationship wasn't the same. Sarah never asked Max to leave his girlfriend to be with her. She felt if he wanted to be with her, he would. Every now and then, Sarah would come home and find an envelope full of money Max pushed underneath her back door for her and Hannah. Even though she wasn't talking to Max, she used the money he gave to pay her bills, not that she needed his help, but because he offered. She felt this was his way of paying her back for what he did. A couple of months had gone by, and Sarah was sure she wasn't going to talk to Max anymore or accept anything he had to offer, until she got a call from Max saying he was leaving his ex. Sarah could care less about him leaving her. That was before she received a voice message from his ex-girlfriend saying that she was tired of Max. He was there with her, but his heart was with Sarah. She said she put him out and Sarah could have him. Sarah was standing firm on not seeing Max ever again. She didn't want to be a part of a love triangle; however, Max did everything he could to change her mind. And he did. The calls from Max's ex-girlfriend had stopped completely. Max got his number changed to prove to Sarah that he was done with his ex-girlfriend. Max and Sarah started back talking, and she fell in love with Max all over again as if she never fell out of love with him. Sarah moved out of her apartment and later closed on her first house. It was a brick bungalow located in the north county area of St. Louis. It was the perfect starter home and exceptional neighborhood to raise their daughters, Hannah who was five years of age and their daughter, Haven, who was on the way. With their dreadful past behind them, Sarah and Max could finally move forward. Max moved in completely shortly after Sarah gave birth to Haven. Like many relationships, they experienced highs and lows. Undeniable challenges shook the very ground they stood on. Sarah was not familiar with Max's profession as a Journeyman Ironworker other than what he had told her, but she was soon to find out.

Max didn't complete Sarah; he was a bonus to her already fruitful life, although she felt incomplete when he wasn't around. They were like hot water and steam. He was the water to her pond that she hoped would never run dry. He loved her, she loved him, and no one could say different. Max and Sarah did everything together. He was the first man she ever truly loved, her first official boyfriend. Because of the feelings Sarah and Max had for one another, one could only imagine what it led to. Sarah refrained from going to the store, visiting friends, parks and parties, or doing anything without Max by her side. She couldn't sleep without him either. She developed an obsession for Max that neither one of them understood. It didn't occur to her how this obsession took her life and pushed it into a dark tunnel in hopes to never see the light again, until one day, her actions revealed the lack of self-control she never possessed.

Max decided instead of coming home first after work, he'd go out with some friends. What drove Sarah crazy the most was the fact that Max didn't come home first to check on his family. She awaited text and phone calls of his whereabouts and got nothing. Max stayed out past his nine o'clock p.m. curfew. They both agreed that if they were not together, that they would be in the house no later than nine o'clock p.m. This was excellent and logical since they were always together. Sarah called Max's phone throughout the night in hopes he would answer. She allowed her emotions to take over her logical way of thinking. Max didn't call back. Sarah sent Max several text messages.

"Where are you?"

"I can't believe you are not here."

"You're no good."

"I can't believe you. There's no telling what you are out there doing."

"I can't stand you right now. You make me sick to my stomach."

Sarah allowed this unhealthy behavior of texting and calling Max to drag on until his phone start going straight to voicemail.

Sarah's mind began to wander.

"Sarah," the woman laughed menacingly. "he will always come back to me."

Boom! The slamming of Max's truck door broke Sarah's daydream. She looked at the time on her phone. 1:14AM. Max walked into the house, looking straight ahead as he made his way to the bedroom. Sarah gathered her thoughts and stormed into the room behind him. She wasted no time telling him everything he wasn't. Her intentions were to tear him down emotionally beyond repair.

Max looked at Sarah and said, "I never go anywhere." He raised his voice before regaining control of his temper. "I go to work, and I come home! At least I come home. I'm not out cheating!" He yelled. He thought briefly about the times he didn't come home. He hoped that him letting go of his double life would make Sarah happy. "Some of the guys ask me to go out for drinks after work, and I did."

Sarah stared at him as he got undressed. She rolled her eyes then left him to be alone after he spoke the truth about him never going anywhere. She went into the front room to reflect on all the things she did and said.

Sarah had a one on one with herself as she paced the floor. *I could have handled this situation better, but he knew to come home first.* She walked into the kitchen and start putting the dishes in the sink into the kitchen cabinet and talking softly to herself: "I'll admit, I was wrong on so many levels, but I wasn't going to tell him that. I don't approve of him staying out late coming home at one o'clock in the morning." She stomped down the stairs into the laundry room. "Please! That's a new day. You didn't come home." She opened the dryer door and threw the clothes into the laundry basket. "If I let it slide this time, then he's going to keep on doing it." Sarah chose to stand her ground that night, falling to sleep on the couch.

Max came into the living room and carried Sarah to their bedroom.

After that long memorable night, Sarah realized breaking her obsession with Max was mandatory. She called her life coach and God-sister, Lisa. Sarah had known Lisa since she was a preteen. She showed her how to be a mother to Hannah. She helped her become a woman. She pushed Sarah to finish school when others said she should quit and get a job to take care of Hannah. Sarah turned to Lisa for helpful advice when she was backed up against the rope and it became difficult for her to bounce back. Sarah learned to learn from others' mistakes. She told her sister everything that happened last night. Lisa took both sides.

"Sarah I know how you feel. I've been there, Lisa explained. "I also know how you made Max feel. I've been on both sides of the fence, and trust me when I say it's not easy. I experienced that very same attachment with my husband."

"You never told me that."

"That's not something you just tell. What did you want me to say? I'm making myself miserable? I have thrown away my life to be a part of his? Be for real."

"Yeah, I guess. So what do I do now? Now that we have identified the heart-wrenching problem?"

"Well, in order to get over one obsession, you have to find a new one. You have to wean yourself off of Max. Keep in mind, it's a process, so you must do so slowly. If you attempt to do it overnight, you're just going to relapse and make it worse. Look at it like a drug. If people don't get the proper help and take the appropriate steps, they end up going back to drugs; some addicts have even overdosed."

Sarah awaited in-depth instructions.

"You have to refrain from spending so much time with him. Instead of movie night with him, go out with friends."

Sarah pushed everyone that was close to her away. When her friends hosted something, she would be the first to know and the only one to not show because she didn't want to leave Max's side. Eventually, her friends stop calling. Sarah thought that following Lisa's advice would be easier said than done.

However, at this point, she was desperate for a change, so she immediately took Lisa's advice. She reconnected with her friends and family. Sarah's real friends accepted her without holding anything against her after months of no communication. They refrained from asking her anything about her and Max's relationship.

Lauren arranged a special girl's night out for Sarah. They met at the Law's Bar and Grill for karaoke night. She enjoyed being around her friends. Even though she wasn't with Max physically, her mind was. She felt like a stalker-- nothing physical only mental. Lauren had never seen Sarah so caught up in a relationship. In fact, she's never seen Sarah in a relationship. She knew Sarah refused to be tied down. Sarah ran through men like she ran through clothes. She didn't sleep around with the guys she messed with. She used them for what they had to offer until they wanted something from her in return; then she'll disappear on them. Lauren could tell Sarah changed, but she wasn't sure if Sarah's change was a good one. Lauren invited Sarah, Hannah, and Haven to join her in attending her aunt's annual church picnic the following weekend. Lauren thought this event would help with Sarah's transition. Sarah was unsure at the time if she would attend, so she told Lauren she would consider going if Max didn't make plans for them.

Sarah never told Max she was sorry for flipping out that night, but she attempted to show him she was sorry by going back to her regular routine of cooking, cleaning, and making sure he had everything he needed before work like nothing happened. Max accepted that and returned to his regular routine as well. On the third day of the week, Sarah spoke to Max to see if he had made any plans for them over the weekend. He told her that he had a lot of things to do around the house, so he wouldn't be able to do anything outside of housework.

After much deliberation, Sarah, Hannah, and Haven attended Lauren's aunt's annual church picnic, given that Lauren wasn't taking no for an answer. While enjoying the picnic, Lauren introduced Sarah to a lot of wonderful, loving people who kept smiles on their faces. Sarah was sitting at a picnic table talking to Lauren when Lauren's aunt Martha sat down beside her. Sarah had known Martha about as long as she knew Lauren. Martha was a sweet God-fearing woman who cherished Sarah as her own daughter. Martha talked to Sarah about a garment business she just joined. Martha knew Sarah was business minded, and this company would be of great interest to her. She was right. After Martha finish explaining the company process to Sarah, she was ready to start. She saw this as a good item to add to her clothing business she had the plan to operate. It would be additional income to put in her bank account. Martha gave Sarah detailed information about the next business meeting. Sarah hugged Martha and thanked her for the opportunity. Then she excused herself to go check on Hannah, who was running around with the other kids having fun. Sarah put Haven in the swing and pushed her gently. A short man wearing sunglasses came over to Sarah and stood beside the swing. He introduced himself saying his name was Bishop Edwards. He was the overseer of the church, a pretty good one from what Sarah was told. He thanked Sarah for coming and invited her to Sunday morning worship. She agreed to come. She didn't know of anyone who would turn down an invite to attend a church, especially after one of her kids ate everything they saw and the other one made a mess by playing in their food. She thought it was only right to accept the invitation. It wasn't as though she had never been to church. When she was little, she and her little sister, Evans, attended a big Catholic Church by themselves. The church was walking distance from their home. Sarah recalled herself and her siblings getting up early so her mother could do their hair for church and sitting on her knees at the altar during communion.

The following morning, Sarah prepared breakfast before getting dressed to attend Sunday service at Bishop Edwards' church.

She knew that getting invited to attend church that Sunday wasn't a coincidence. If no one else knew she was walking on her tippy toes trying to stay afloat because the ground was crumbling beneath her feet, God knew.

It wasn't long before Max realized Sarah wouldn't be joining him for his traditional Sunday football watching.

"Hey, where are you all going so early?" Max asked.

Sarah cleared her throat and smiled. "To Lauren's church."

"Lauren goes to church?" Max smirked. "I would have never thought she did."

"Well, she doesn't go all the time. It's her auntie's church."
Sarah wasn't expecting Max to accompany them.

Max kissed Sarah on the cheek. "Have fun! I'll see you
when you get home." Max lay down on the couch.

Sarah had driven thirty minutes before she arrived at the
church. She had no problem finding it because service was
being held in an unusual place: her old middle school
auditorium. Sarah was greeted with a much-needed big smile
and a warm hug that she wasn't expecting once she arrived at
the church. Sarah, Hannah, and Haven sat in the back of the
church because she didn't know anyone there. Lauren hardly
ever came to church, forsaking to assemble, but she was there
for every church picnic, concert, and vacation. Sarah never
understood why Lauren did that; she participated in everything
the church had, but when it came to Sunday worship, giving
God thanks for making all those things possible, she was a no
show.

Sarah enjoyed herself at church. She felt that God was
talking directly to her. She was amazed and drawn into the
church because of the love they expressed. Bishop Edwards let
her know he was glad that she came. She attended many
churches, but none of them could compare to this church. He
made her feel important and loved when he acknowledged her
by name. He did a corporate prayer, asking God to draw her
into becoming a member of his church.

When Sarah got home, Max asked her about church. She
told him she really enjoyed herself, and she was looking
forward to attending next Sunday. The next Sunday, Sarah
showed up at the church after praise and worship. As she sat
attempting to listen to Bishop Edwards preach, all she could
think about was Max not being there with her and her new
clothing company. She brought her business mind into the
church. She saw everyone as a potential client. She wondered if
there was such thing as church clientele. Her thoughts of
building an empire based on church clientele were shattered
through the message Bishop Edwards was preaching.

"Some people come to church to profit from people in the church." Bishop Edwards yelled as he looked over the crowd.

Sarah looked around.

"They have brought their stinking thinking into the church."

Sarah crossed her legs before looking over at her children.

"Instead of relying on people to make you successful, you should develop a relationship with God who will give you the desires of your heart. He will bring you to the land flowing with milk and honey. No good thing will he withhold from you."

After service, some of the members ask Sarah where did she get her dress.

"I got it made," She smirked.

"You sell clothes, " asked a member. She walked around Sarah looking at her dress.

"Yes."

"How much? I want one of these."

"Fifteen dollars."

"Fifteen dollars for a dress. Girl... It's cute though." The woman walked away.

Sarah remembered what Bishop Edwards said about coming into the church just to do business. Sarah went home and laid under Max and waited until he was finished cooking.

Sarah had a hard time separating church from the outside world. She felt as though her sins would always be revealed whenever the word went forth, whether it was physical fornication before or after service, a mental fornication during service, cursing, or failing to love someone other than the people in her inner circle. Even after feeling beat up spiritually around the clock, she wasn't willing to give up so easily. She attended the church five weeks in a row.

On the sixth Sunday of her attending church, Sarah went expecting to leave different from when she first came. She tuned in to Elder Mittens who was standing at the podium. She sat comfortably amongst others as the word went forth.

"You can't keep waiting for your mama, daddy, boyfriend, and them to get saved; you must first save yourself," Elder Mittens bellowed across the pulpit.

Sarah desperately wanted to wait for Max to come to church so they could get saved together. Many times she envisioned them holding hands walking together down to the altar to surrender to God, but she was instantly reminded by her thoughts of Max's ex-girlfriend telling her that she and Max would never go to church together after she got a hold to a letter Sarah wrote and gave Max. In fact, he wouldn't go at all. "You all would never be happy together," she said on a voice message she left Sarah.

As the season was promised to change, Max stayed the same and never attended church with Sarah. She figured she already experimented with pleasures and enjoyed herself with the things of this world; she had nothing to lose. The world couldn't do anything for her compared to what God would. She believed he created her and predestined her for greatness. Truth is that Sarah knew she wanted to get saved the first day she attended this church, even with her struggles. She could hear God so clearly. Her soul was leaping toward the altar with full force. However, her mind accompanied by her flesh that wouldn't allow her feet to move. It was as though she had put on fifty extra pounds; she could forget about nudging.

The enemy didn't make it any easier. He whispered in her ear. "Everybody is watching you."

He led her to believe that, "If you walk down to the altar, the other people would see how dirty and sinful you are, not hesitating to pass judgment on you."

With everything she was thinking, Sarah resisted the devil by applying adhesive tape to his mouth. She followed the pathway down to the elders and allowed God to save her because she was certain she needed Him. She was fed up with the madness that had moved into her life, cluttering anything she considered to be sane. The elders escorted Sarah to a secluded room in the church.

"Ok, Sarah I want you to call on Jesus," the elder said. You're going to lose control of your tongue once you call on him. You will not be able to stop. Don't be afraid when you're speaking. It's a form of communication between you and God. The enemy can't understand it."

Sarah immediately became afraid to go through with it. She knew that having the Holy Spirit was something she needed to help with her walk with Christ, her guide to keep her on a straight narrow path as she ran this race for Christ. She reminded herself that everyone who runs in a race runs to win, but only one runner gets the prize. She recognized she must run like them so that she can win. The Holy Spirit was the comforter she'd long for and desperately needed, a friend that would always tell her the truth, no matter how it made her feel. He would hold her accountable for her actions while leading her to do the right thing, ensuring that she doesn't allow anyone to hinder her. The Holy Spirit will keep her focus on the things that lay ahead when she finds herself thinking about the things that happen in her past.

Sarah finally surrendered and called on Jesus, and she was thrilled she did. She spoke to Him in tongues for a long time, and turned out she had a lot to talk to Him about. She felt the enormous weight that had piled up on her over the previous years being lifted as she called on Jesus. The more she called on him, the better she felt. He washed away her sins, and she became a new creature. God was now her right hand and no devil in hell could shake her by telling her anything different. The way God made her feel that day replaced any other feelings she had ever experienced in her life. She promised she'd be forever indebted to him. One of the elders pulled Sarah to the side and showed her in the Bible what she experienced.

The elder read aloud. "Acts 2:2, when the Pentecost, the fiftieth day after Passover, came all the believers were together in one place. Suddenly, a sound like a violently blowing wind came from the sky and filled the whole house where they were staying. Tongues that looked like fire appeared to them. The tongue arranged themselves so that one came to rest on each believer. All the believers were filled with the Holy Spirit and began to speak in the other languages as the Spirit gave them the ability to speak."

Sarah pondered. *Surely this is a gift from God that all saints should have. It's not a gift he gives to certain people, but all who believe; God does not play favoritism.*

Given the change Sarah made in her life, Sunday service and Bible study became mandatory for her. She felt the Sunday service alone wasn't enough. She wanted to know about God. Who is He? Why did He die for her? Who was she that He is mindful of her? Her desire to know God became prominent. Weeks followed by months went by, and still no Max. She eventually stopped asking him to accompany them on Sundays. She changed the way she viewed her life: those in it, and the direction it was headed. Every day she prayed, asking God for wisdom, and to create in her a clean heart so that her thoughts and actions be acceptable to Him. The more she converted according to God's will, the more unstable her life seemed.

Late into the evening one day, Sarah came home from work. She was pooped from a busy work day and was looking forward to watching a little television until she couldn't keep her eyes open. She was looking forward to seeing Max when he got home, but she wasn't looking forward to the insane game of "guess what mood I'm in". Sarah didn't notice Max's sudden mood change prior to her getting saved. God began revealing things to Sarah she never knew. She remembered that the only day that brought Max joy during a hectic work week was payday, but she noticed lately it seemed as if he had an entirely different attitude about it. Sarah couldn't understand how a person who made so much money could be so depressed about it. When Max got home, he spoke to Sarah and sat down on the couch. The television station was on ESPN, the same channel he left it on before he left to go to work that morning.

Sarah walked over to Max. She gave him a kiss and handed him the opened mail. Max sat the letter beside him and continued to watch television. Once his show went on commercial, he went through the mail.

"Bills, Bills. Man these bills are high. I can't keep any money." He sighed, tossing the bills on the table beside him.

Sarah braced herself for what was about to happen. She could feel Max's rage push its way towards to the surface.

"Are you going to have any free money when you get paid this week?" Max voice was filled with frustration.

"I have to pay daycare and my truck note. Why? What's wrong?"

"I need you to start helping me out with these bills." He looked over at Sarah. "If you can, skip your truck note this week, and I'll pay it next week."

"If I don't pay it this week, it will be late, and I don't like to be late on my bills." Sarah retorted calmly.

Sarah knew the importance of paying her bills on time to avoid late fees and to keep her credit in good standing. She worked so hard to build her credit so she could buy her first house.

"You are always broke," Max scoffed, looking back at the TV. "Why do you go to work?" He made a disgruntled face.

"The same reason you go to work," Sarah raised her voice a little and took a deep breath. "to make a living." She glanced at the ten-day disconnection notice lying beside Max.

"I'm the only one paying bills around here." He snapped. "You wouldn't be able to afford this place or the bills that come with it without me."

Sarah could feel her stomach turning flips like an acrobat.

"I guess you are content where you are in life. You don't want to do better?" Max shook his head with disappointment.

Max's behavior was unorthodox. Sarah couldn't believe Max was talking to her this way. The argument became very intense and mind-boggling. She couldn't endure the way he was making her feel. Max pierced her mind, heart, and soul with his negative words. His words truly cut deeper than a two-edged sword. He left Sarah questioning her charisma and womanhood. The more he talked, the less likely she could diminish the hurtful words (seeds) he planted. She tried to prevent his words from residing in her mind, spirit, and heart while they waited for the perfect time to torment her.

Sarah suffered in silence. She was thinking about a way to get back at Max without saying anything hurtful to him. She believed actions would overrule words any day.

She proceeded to strategize among herself. *I never felt fulfillment in playing tit for tat; it's very childish and beneath me. However, given what's at stake, someone has to be an adult in this situation. But not me, not today anyway...maybe tomorrow after I made a memorable scene that would play over and over in Max's mind like a carousel ride. I'm convinced this will make him think twice before he disrespected me again.*

Sarah went into the bathroom to take a quick shower. After getting out, she hurried into their bedroom to get dressed. She put on the dress Max bought her about a month ago just because he was thinking of her; he did that often. He said he knew that Sarah would look great in it, and he was right. She believed this dress has become both of their favorite. The dress pushed her confidence into overdrive. It was a fitted black dress with long sleeves, fitting closely to her body, uplifting her bust and flattening her stomach. It hugged her thighs like a magnet and stopped above her knee giving her a bombshell body figure. In other words, she was a brick house built to last forever, enduring the most horrific weather, not easily broken, and would leave an unforgettable impression on you if you ever caused her to fall. The dress was not revealing at all. It did wonders for Max's imagination. It's not what a man sees that makes him want a woman, but it's what he can't see. Men love a mystery and don't want to have to compete with other men's roaming eyes. She wore her show-stopping Hannah Pumps that she purchased from her favorite online shoe store, Uniquedestinyshoes.com. The pumps had a beautiful cheetah print accompanied by a gold and cheetah print strap that embraced her ankle, giving her added support. If you saw her wearing them, you would have never thought that they were only forty bucks. She felt she would have been insane to pass them up. She covered her neck with a thick gold Egyptian style necklace. She put on multiple gold bracelets. She wore a pair of gold dangling earrings. She flat ironed her hair that gave it a beautiful shine and much-needed volume. She enhanced her already fascinating lips by applying a clear lip gloss. She sprayed on Max's favorite perfume, Britney Spears.

She peeped into their girls' bedroom to ensure they were still sleeping; she didn't want them to see her leave. That would be the day she had to lie to them about where she was going. That would have been a red flag in her what not to do as a parent *Parenting 101* magazine. Insuring she caught Max's attention, she switched fearlessly past Max while cutting her eyes at him. She awaited his reaction. She was sure he would ask her, "where she was going dress like that?" Still aggravated and silent, Max continued to sit on their black leather love seat with his feet propped up on the ottoman watching Sports Center. He displayed a look that could strike a match. Unfortunately, Sarah was the target. She purposely grabbed his car keys from off the top of the TV stand instead of hers in hopes to make him a little angrier than he already was. She pushed the automated starter on the truck and stormed out the front door slamming the door behind her. She hoped the disturbing noise didn't wake Hannah and Haven. She walked to the truck. She pulled up on the truck to get in and hopped onto the seat. She took her time sorting through Max's maintenance man like key ring. The vehicle passenger door opened rapidly.

"Hey!"

Sarah screamed.

"What is all that for?"

"Girl, you scared me. The devil's timing is always accurate," Sarah mumbled.

Evans began to question Sarah's motives. "Why are you

dressed up? Where are you going at this time of night? I know they are not holding communion at the church; it's midnight. The only thing that is open this late is the club. Hmm." Evans turned up her lip.

"And Walmart," Sarah smiled. "What's with the fifty questions? I don't remember putting my hand on the Bible to take an oath. Where's the trial and why I am I on it? The last time I checked my mother's name was Pamela, not Evans."

"Girl bye! You have always been extra. You didn't have to say all that." She shook her head.

"Let me guess: you and Max just had a fight. That's good-- well, not for him. Now you have a reason to go out with me. I was just coming by to borrow your red pumps, your earrings-- oh, and that black dress, but I see you have it on." Evans examined Sarah from head to toe and shook her head with disappointment.

"Girl, I'm not going out with you. You know I don't do clubs anymore." Sarah said staring at Evans.

"Oh yeah, that's right. You're saved and ready to testify. I'm not surprised you said that. Saved people kill me. They are always looking down on somebody just because they are not saved. I guess you have forgotten how we used to club 'til six in the morning. I see you got a man now. You don't know how to act, and you still haven't answered my question. Where is Ms. Holier than thou going at this time of night? You know what momma use to say. There're only two things open at this time of the night. You just said you are not going to the club so that leaves the other thing." Evans grinned. "Awe, you cheating?"

Sarah turned her head quickly in disbelief that she would even fix her mouth to say that. "No! Why would I do that?"

"Uh, you know why. I know. I would, shoot." Sarah's response wasn't sitting too well with Evans given everything she knew.

"Let me clear something up," Sarah started, " God gave me the mindset to stop going to the club long before I became saved. Getting saved was icing on the cake. Don't go judging people. All church people don't look down on the unsaved. I don't. I haven't forgotten where I came from. God made me realize that the things I once did led me straight to Him. I'm happy. I have a man that loves me and only me. Did you catch that?"

Evans sat in silence.

"Girl, get out of my truck I'm late for my date with Walmart."

"Really, that's where you're going dressed like that? Who you are trying to pick up Mr. Clean?" Evans laughed.

"No, I'm just going to clear my head. Good-bye. You are holding me up." Sarah opened the truck door and pushed Evans out of the truck.

Evans laughed. "Girl, you are saved for real."

Sarah drove off and started her commute to Walmart. She called Lauren.

"Hello?"

"What are you doing?"

"Sleep. I have to go to work in the morning. Some people actually do labor on their jobs. What are you doing up? Why does it sound like you're driving?" Lauren was concerned.

"Because I am." Sarah laughed.

"What?"

"Hey, did you get that picture I sent to your phone not too long ago?" Sarah checked her picture mail to insure it was sent correctly. "Wait a minute." Lauren looked at her incoming messages.

"Oh, that's cute. Wait, you're wearing that now?" She was surprised.

"Yes."

Lauren thought about what Sarah said. "OK, where are you going? But most importantly, where is Max?"

"He's at home with our kids. He is most likely looking crazy. I'm on my way to Walmart. I wanted him to think I was going somewhere else, so I dressed up and left. I had to switch it up with him because usually I just get mad for a little while, then I am the one who apologizes."

Lauren was at a loss for words.

"So I left. I had to let him know I don't play games. I dropped out of school because of recess. He hasn't even called me. He's such a bombastic jerk. I was more upset with him because he didn't call me to show that he was a little concern."

"Oh Lord! Girl how long have you been gone now?"

"Not that long. About an hour."

"Girl take your butt back home. Makeup. Make love. Do something with the word make in it. Call me tomorrow. Wait, call me later today," Lauren yawned. "Make sure you text me to let me know you made it home safe."

"I'm already home. I've been driving around the neighborhood since I left home. I didn't want to look crazy walking around Walmart dress like I am a Vegas showgirl looking for a good time. Plus, these shoes hurt my feet." Sarah was reaping the pain from her uncomfortable shoes. She felt as though her toes were working together to break free. She immediately forced them off her feet.

"Ok, bye girl"

Sarah sat in the truck a little while longer. She took that time to talk to God.

It took some time for Sarah to embrace the change of being saved, especially with her friends withdrawing from her now saved lifestyle. The more she talked to God and did things His way, the more she found him blessing her. Sarah was ecstatic that God was willing to do so much for her after all she has done. She embraced the breeze of blessings, but she had no idea of the storm that followed that was carrying many lessons.

Max was coming home a little later than usual, yet Sarah didn't say anything. She knew something wasn't right. She had hoped for the best. Although, she couldn't lose sight of the fact that Max had a bad problem. When she meet Max, it seemed he had this problem under control. She preferred to never get involved with what he was doing. Luckily he had stopped this problem before Sarah got saved, so that was one thing she didn't have to worry about— or so she thought. Bishop Edwards had been teaching on discernment, a women's intuition. Sarah exercised her judgment when it came to Max.

Sarah was going through the kitchen drawer when she came across Max's bank statement. It had several different transactions that didn't make sense to her. There were at least seven ATM charges of two dollars and fifty cents. There were twenty charges overall for the month. Sarah waited irritably until Max got home from work to discuss what she saw on his bank account. Outside their house around nine o'clock p.m., Sarah heard Max's truck pulling into the driveway. Sarah was sitting on the couch, attempting to watch TV when Max put the key into the door.

"Hey honey," Max smiled as he opened the front door to come into the house.

"Hey," she smirked.

"Where are the kids?" Max asked closing the door behind him.

"In the bed."

"How's it going baby doll?" He walked over and kissed Sarah on the cheek.

"Not good." Sarah shook her head in disbelief. "I guess the saying is true: what's done in the dark will come to light." Sarah gave Max an unpleasant look.

"What do you mean by that, babe? What's wrong?" Max sat down on the couch across from Sarah.

"Can I ask you something?" she said while she stared at the TV.

"Sure, baby, you can ask me anything." Max briefly searched his thoughts for an explanation for Sarah's untimely conduct.

She looked at him then back at the TV. "Are you still gambling?"

"Why you ask me that?" Max took a deep swallow and didn't move a muscle.

"I've been wondering why the casino keeps mailing you prizes and gifts."

"They always do that." He began sweating.

"Ok, I see you are not going to answer my question. So I'll hit the ground running." She tilted her head and slightly poked her lip out. "I found your bank statement in the drawer. Normally I don't look at them, but this time I did. I saw several ATM charges. I couldn't understand why you would keep going to the ATM, withdrawing money knowing the fees were so high".

Max dropped his head and swallowed.

"Then it hit me. The same day you received all those charges was the same day you weren't answering your phone when I called. The only time you don't answer your phone is when you're on the job where you can't answer, or you are doing something you have no business doing, like at the casino gambling."

"Now hold up! Let me stop you right there," Max raised his voice. "What are you doing checking behind me? If I want to spend my money on the boat, I can. I work hard for my money. I can do what I want. I'm not about to sit here and let you tell me otherwise." Max got up and went into the kitchen.

"Oh, so I'm wrong here?" Sarah pointed to herself and walking behind Max. "Did you forget you're the reason the house is in foreclosure and the bills are behind?" Sarah folded her arms. "There's no way we should be broke with the kind of money you make." Sarah shouted.

"You act like it's all me. You work too. Where is your money going?" He raised his voice. "You shop, shop, shop!" Max pulled the shopping bags from underneath the kitchen cabinet and threw them on the floor.

Sarah thought to herself, *I hope he knows I'm not picking them bags up while he is throwing them everywhere.*

Sarah argued to get to the bottom of this depressing behavior. "That's a lie and you know it. I buy what is needed to survive. Sometimes I don't pay things because you agree to pay them saying 'baby don't worry about the bills, I'll take care of it.' I don't make that much money on my job, and you know that!" Sarah stared into Max eyes.

"Now that I think about it, you don't really shop a lot; the money I did give you, you spent on that little problem you had." said Max. He looked at Sarah. "Why are you still working there if you are not making any money? What are you working for, just to say you have a job?" Max studied Sarah as he talked. "I have a career; I been telling you for almost three years to come off your job so I can take care of you, but you want to be Ms. Independent. How is that working for you? You acting like you don't need me."

"First, let's clear this up," Sarah rolled her eyes and cleared her throat. "I don't need you! I was perfectly fine when you met me. I had a house, truck, and a job. I paid my bills on time, and had good credit. Do I need to say more? I allowed you to be a part of my life and help me where you saw fit. Don't every think for a second I can't do without you. That's when I'll be tempted to prove you wrong!" Sarah arranged the books sitting on the kitchen counter. "What does that have to do with anything 'you have a career?'" I'm working towards mine! You are thirty-two! I would hope you have one. My job has nothing to do with this situation. We're talking about you, your job, and your habits that's bringing us down.

Max stared into the other room, hoping Sarah would shut up already. "To make matters worse, you got bronchitis from going on the boat, and you don't even smoke. Who does that? You know what? I'm just going to tell you like this. I have never been a fan of gambling and I never will. I can't see how people work so hard for their money then go give it away, but not in a good way. It's not like you giving it away to help someone." She watched Max as he stared at the wall. "You go play stupid games that are designed to take your money and leave you depressed. I remember when you use to come home from work and show me how much money you made for that pay period."

Max swallowed and shook his head as he thought back on those days.

"Then you would turn around the next day and it would be gone."

Max looked at Sarah. He hated everything she was saying. "I would have to give you money to get you back and forth to work, get myself to work, and take the kids to separate schools. Oh, by the way, I did that with my low paying job you have been strong-mindedly trying to remove me from. I never said anything because I didn't know what to say or how to say it. I would just pray about it." She walked to the table and placed her hand on it.

"I remember that day you stayed out all night without calling." Max took a deep breath.

"When you got home, you were pouting, telling me that you lost your entire paycheck, but you made some of it back, and you gave me five hundred dollars. Then you ask me if I could come up with the rest of the money to pay bills. If I didn't have any money, I would go to friends and family for help."

Max rubbed the back of his head. He looked at the clock on the microwave.

"They never said anything or questioned me about the money until I guess it was obvious that something was wrong." Max sat down at the kitchen table.

"Things wasn't adding up." Sarah looked at the bank statement lying on the couch.

"My brother asked me, why are you always broke and Max claim to make so much money?'"

"I was too embarrassed to tell him. Plus, my mother always taught us that whatever goes on in your house is your business, and it should never leave your house, unless you were being abused. Therefore, I just said, 'he's not working every day.' I convinced myself that I couldn't do it anymore. I was tired of being a slave to the lender. I recall you telling me you were going to stop gambling."

Max looked up at Sarah with a sense of desperation.

"I guess you did stop for a little while, but now I see you have been sneaking around doing it." Sarah shook her head.

She walked into the living room and turned off the tv.

Max stood up and faced Sarah. "So what now?"

She stared at him as if he said nothing. She took a deep breath and swallowed. She looked at him then looked away. "I can't do this anymore." She said softly." I refuse to."

"What do you mean?" Max heart pounded.

"You talk about how ironworkers make all this money and they blow it on hookers and liquor, drugs, and all that, what makes you any different? Those are all considered bad habits (addictions). They take away from your finances and state of mind. At least they get something from it. The person who pays for hookers gets sex. The person who drinks or do drugs can wash away his problems for a little while. What do you have to show for your gambling? Nothing but disappointment, overdue bills, and a woman that's ready to cut ties with you. I will not sit back while you hurt me and the kids with your stupid habits." Sarah straighten the pillows on the couch. "I refuse to relive my childhood in my home. If this is what you want to do, then fine, but count me out." She looked at Max. He was leaning on the wall in the kitchen.

"I'm not going to live like this. I will leave you quicker than your money does on the casino."

Max didn't know what to say. He couldn't fix his lips to even say I'm sorry. So he just stood there looking at Sarah as she picked up toys from off the floor. Sarah wasn't expecting a response from Max; she didn't want one. After she cleaned the front room, she took a long shower before going to bed.

Sarah monitored Max's depressing habit for several weeks. She prayed without ceasing. Without even realizing it, her prayers had been answered; months had gone by and Max hadn't gambled. His bank statements was clean of outrageous casino ATM charges. The casino gift cards and brochures stopped coming in the mail. Max desired to keep Sarah in his life more than he desired to feed his sick gambling obsession. Now that was out the way, Max focused on making sure Sarah was stationary in his life. He knew if he ask her for the sixth time to marry him she would say yes.

Early Saturday morning, Max woke Sarah up by tapping her on the shoulder. He informed her that he was going grocery shopping. If it was any other given day, month and year, she would have told him, "HECK NO, you can't go"; however, a lot has changed, including her. She knew he was an early bird; plus, Shop-n-Save was open twenty-four hours a day. Sarah laid back down, pulling the comforter over her head, embracing the warmth it projected as she resumed the cuddle session between her and her cover. When Max left, so many thoughts ran throughout her head: *could he be cheating? He didn't even make out a grocery list.*

To prevent her mind from exploding with unanswered questions she generated, Sarah turned on some gospel music and started cleaning up around the house. Five hours into the day, Max arrived home. Sarah became nervous as she always does when she's around Max, as if they had just met, and she didn't know what to expect of him. Max kissed Sarah on the back of her neck. He raised her shirt and kissed her softly on her lower back. Sarah enthusiastically turned around to find Max kneeling on his right knee. He smiled while holding a wrinkled paper bag in his hand telling her to reach inside. Already feeling nervous, she reached inside the bag. She pulled out a small square black box.

"Before you open it," Max smiled. "I want to hand you my heart. A lot of times I just sit and ask myself what could you possibly see in me because you're so beautiful inside and out. You can have any man that you want, but you choose to be with me despite my stupidity and inability to make the right choices at times. You deserve everything you desire, and I want to be the one to give it to you. I promised myself that I wouldn't do this again, but you changed my mind. I love you with all my heart. Your face is the last thing I want to see at night and the very first thing I want to embrace in the morning for the rest of our life. Sarah Renee Strive, will you marry me?."

"Can I open it?"

He smiled happily. "Yes, you can open it."

"Yes!" Sarah smiled jumping up and down. She gave Max a big hug. She opened the box.

"Aw, baby." Sarah started crying as Max removed the ring from the box and placed it on her finger. She smiled and placed her hand onto her chest as she admired the sliver band ring with a small diamond in the middle.

Refusing to think twice, the next day Max and Sarah went to the courthouse to get their marriage license in hopes to get married very soon, on a day in which Max didn't have to work. The following week Sarah, Lauren, Evans, Stacey, and Karen went to Allure Bridal to pick out a dress for a milestone Sarah was about to reach in her life. It had taken several visits there before Sarah found the perfect wedding dress. However, she found the bridesmaids and maid of honor dresses with no problem. The ladies put their bridesmaid dress on layaway, and Sarah put her wedding dress in as well. She couldn't wait to tell Max about the perfect dress she found; it was only nine hundred ninety-five dollars after taxes. That wasn't even half of one of Max's weekly paychecks. Of course, there were a lot of cheaper dresses, but a person only gets married once. The dress was stunning; it was nothing like Sarah would have ever dreamed of being able to afford. It was an ivory strapless Jovani gown with an A-line skirt that featured a beautiful flowing train and a sheer illusion sweetheart neckline.

A month had passed, and the name Sarah Strive seemed to remain active and untouched. Sarah stopped by her spiritual parents' place to talk about Max, whom they did not know. They were slightly unaware that she was about to get married, other than the shocking marriage license she posted on Facebook. Given that they were loving, concerned spiritual parents, Bishop Edwards asked to meet Max. Sarah's heart dropped when he told her that.

Sarah thought, *I can't get him to come to church. How in the world will I convince him to meet Bishop Edwards and First Lady Edwards?*

"What's wrong daughter? You don't want me to meet him? I am very protective when it comes to my spiritual daughters. I want to make sure he's out for your best interest and not his own." Bishop Edwards smiled.

Sarah knew he was serious. "Ok, I'll let him know you would like to meet him."

"So what church does he attend?" Bishop Edwards folded his hands and pushed back in his chair.

Sarah smirked before clearing her throat. She became hesitant. "Uh, he doesn't go to church." Sarah wasn't surprised by his question.

"First Lady!" Bishop Edwards yelled into the other room. Bishop Edwards informed First Lady Edwards of their current discussion.

Sarah felt a much-needed teaching approaching.

"Come with me," First Lady Edwards instructed Sarah.

Sarah walked into First Lady Edwards's office and sat down in a chair in front of the desk.

"So you desire to get married." First Lady Edwards reached for her Bible. She got comfortable in her office chair before opening her Bible without hesitation.

Sarah knew she was going to hear something that would alter her decision about Max. She could feel it residing in her gut. The feeling you get when something bad is about to happen.

"Sarah, my daughter." First Lady Edwards flipped through the Bible.

"Yes."

"I'm glad you want to get married. The Bible states it's better to marry than to burn with lust. So I have a question for you: did you find him, or did he find you?"

"He found me," Sarah smiled. That was odd for her because she always preferred to approach the guys she found interesting.

"That's good. The Bible says 'he that finds a wife finds a good thing and receives favor from God'."

Sarah smiled, "I did something right." She mumbled.

"The Bible also says do not be unequally yoked with unbelievers. You love God, you saved, living holy, and the other person can care less who God is. They're not attempting to get saved. You know they're not going to come to church, but don't be fooled. I have seen it plenty of times where the guy comes to church so that the girl would think he changed. He relapses and stop coming to church, but by then there's nothing a woman can do because they're married now. She has to do what her husband says. According to the Bible, the scripture states, wives submit yourselves to your own husband as you do to the Lord. So if you marry him and proclaim to be a child of God, then you have to do what your husband says. Let's say you all get married, and he says, 'look I don't want you to go to that church anymore'. What will you do?"

"I'll still come," Sarah giggled.

"You can't do that; well you can, however you will be out of the will of God. That's why it's crucial to know who you marry because the head of every man is Christ, and the head of the woman is the man, and the head of Christ is God. That's where a lot of women go wrong; they are trying to be the head."

Sarah sat up straight in her seat.

"God made Adam first and put him in control of everything. When God saw that Adam was lonely, he created Eve from Adams's rib, so a woman should never feel like she has no value because she's not the head. She adds much-needed value to their marriage, especially when she stays in her lane. What people fail to understand is when your relationship doesn't line up according to God's manual, you're more than likely going to catch hell.

Sarah swallowed. *That explains all the hell I was going through.*

"There are challenges with maintaining a healthy relationship with two saved people; imagine what it would be like if you're saved and he's not. In other words, when you marry an unbeliever, your father-in-law will be the devil." First Lady looked at Sarah.

Sarah sat with her mouth slightly open, slightly unsure of what First Lady Edwards was saying. "What?"

First Lady went to the scripture to show Sarah what she was talking about.

"Yes. 'If God were your father, you would love me, I proceeded and have come from God, for I have not even come on my own initiative, but he sent me. Why do you not understand what I am saying? It's because you cannot hear my word. You are of your father the devil, and you want to do the desires of your father'."

"Wow, I've never read that scripture like that before." In fact, Sarah can't recall ever reading that scripture. *I need to increase my Bible knowledge,* she thought.

"I remember reading that a man is saved because of his wife, and likewise, the wife is saved by her husband." Sarah tried to justify her marrying Max would be okay.

"It does state that, but that's only if the couple was unbelievers when they got married and one of them started going to church and got saved."

"Oh, ok, but what about--

"Sarah there is no way around this," First Lady Edwards politely interrupted. "If he is not saved and you get married, you will be out of the will of God. And you will surely pay for it in the long run."

"Okay," Sarah sighed, feeling heartbroken and disappointed. Sarah pondered. *What am I going to do now?*

Sarah hugged First Lady Edwards. "Thank you for loving me enough to tell me the truth." Sarah walked toward the door with her head down.

"Hey Sarah, cheer up. Everything will work out fine. If that's the man God has for you to marry, you all will get married God's way. I love you." First Lady Edwards said compassionate.

When Sarah arrived home, she didn't say anything to Max; however, he knew something was wrong with her but didn't know what it was. She sat in the basement and prayed, asking God to give her the right words to tell Max.

Max walked down the basement steps. "Hey, baby doll."

Max kissed Sarah on her forehead. "Why are you sitting down here in the dark?"

"No reason." She sniffled.

"Babe, why are you crying? Is everything ok?" Max wiped her tears with the tip of his sleeve. He cradled her in his arms.

"There's something I have to tell you." Sarah put her head down.

"What is it babe? You can tell me anything." Max raised her chin slowly with his hand, looking into her eyes.

"I love you so much, Max," her voice became shaky as she built up the courage to tell him.

"I love you too, babe. I will always love you, no matter what."

There it was, the opening she needed. "Even if I told you I don't want to get married anymore?" She spoke slowly so she wouldn't have to repeat herself. "Lord help me," She mumbled.

Max jumped up from off the couch pushing Sarah off of him. "What do you mean? We have our marriage license! You just put down five hundred fifty dollars on your wedding dress!" He was furious.

She told him everything that she learned today about marriage minus who told her and that he was the devil's child.

Max looked shocked. "You know what? I don't know who you are anymore. That church has changed you. I went along with not having sex because you said you felt uncomfortable and convicted. It's been two months now. I don't even know what your naked body looks like anymore!" Max stared Sarah up and down. "Do you still have one? You know what? I'm done with you. I'm doing everything to make you happy, and you don't appreciate it. It's always something I'm not doing or could be doing. From now on, don't ask me to do anything! I don't have to marry you. I was doing you a favor. Look at you with your church going, fake shouting, I'm so saved butt. It's funny how you so holy when you're out in public, but when you come home, you quick to get an attitude and say any and everything that comes to mind. You wonder why I don't go to church with you. You haven't changed. It seems you just going to say that you're going. I don't want to be like that. I'm not about to play with God." Max grabbed his keys and rushed upstairs. He moved swiftly out the front door slamming it behind him.

Sarah wondered if Max wanted to rush their marriage so they could go back to having sex, or so she couldn't force him to attend church with her because of his current absence. Of course, Max wanting to move out now was crazy on his part because he had no place to go. They came to the conclusion that they would just stay together until further notice. Max stayed in the basement while the kids and Sarah remained upstairs, carrying out their daily routine as if nothing happen. This only lasted for three weeks. Max would only speak when she spoke to him, or he would say good morning. It took him longer to forgive, whereas Sarah learned life is too short to hold grudges. She knew if she didn't forgive, God wouldn't answer her prayers. With everything going south, she needed her prayers answered. Max understood where Sarah was coming from about not getting married just yet, and he respected the fact that she didn't want to have sex with him. Sarah and her friends couldn't get their money back from the dresses they placed on hold at Allure Bridal. The store gave them store credit, which they later used to help Lauren purchase her dream wedding gown for her upcoming wedding.

When Sarah woke up Sunday morning, the Holy Spirit told her to ask Max if he wanted to go to church. Sarah refused several times. She went into the laundry room to gather clothes for church. She walked upstairs from the basement and noticed Max cooking breakfast.

"Good morning." She said in a dejected tone. She headed toward their bedroom. She sat on the bed feeling spiritually defeated and mentally drained. She wanted to serve God, yet she knew praising him in church and coming home shacking wasn't going to cut it, even though they were no longer having sex. They still stayed in the same house and slept in the same bed. She felt distasteful. Max followed her into the bedroom.

"What are you doing still lying in bed?" Max asked. He was shocked that she wasn't getting ready for church already.

"Why? You're not going with me." Sarah displayed a slight attitude.

"How do you know?" Max gave her a playful smile.

"Stop looking at me like that; you know how that makes me feel. How are you going? You're not even dressed yet," Sarah was doubtful.

The Holy Spirit spoke to her, telling her to get up and get dressed for church, and Max would follow. Sarah obeyed. However, she didn't bother to check to see if Max was behind her once she had gotten dressed. Her heart couldn't take any more disappointments from him. She opened the front door to step outside. She felt a light tap on her shoulder. She turned around.

"So you were just going to leave without me?" Max smiled. "How do I look?" He stepped back.

"You look good." Sarah smiled while crying internally.

They arrived at the church before praise and worship. For Sarah, service was more fulfilling than ever. Often times during church services, her mind wasn't entirely focused on the word going forth, but on Max. She was too worried about him. She was pleased that she didn't have to this time because he was right next to her. Sarah introduced Max to Bishop Edwards and First lady Edwards after service.

Max didn't say much about church other than he could relate to what Bishop Edwards preached about. Once they made it home Sarah allowed Max to speak freely about what was on his mind

"I don't like your Bishop." Max expressed his unforeseen thoughts.

"What! Why not? you don't even know him." Sarah became angered that he would say such a thing.

Max walked off silent, not wanting to talk about it. Sarah didn't say anything; she knew that was something she needed to pray about. There was nothing she could have said to make him like Bishop Edwards. She became cautious of what spiritual battles she chose to fight. She handed the ones she had no control over to God, like this one.

The following Sunday, Sarah anticipated Max's presence. However, she wasn't surprised that he didn't go, given the comment he made last Sunday. She wasn't discouraged by Max not going to church.

Sarah unrelentingly went to church for herself because she knew no one can win God's favor on her behalf. She had to do it herself. Despite her disapproval of Max not going to church, she treated him as if he was her future king and never mentioned church again. She avoided getting into arguments with him, reflecting back on the comment he made saying, "she hasn't changed." He was calling her a white robe wearing sinner with stains Oxyclean couldn't get out. She avoided getting angry in front of him. If she failed at not getting angry, she made sure she didn't sin. She didn't allow it to consume her. It seemed Max took notice. He refrained form starting arguments with Sarah. Sarah took advantage of Bishop Edwards' Bible teachings and applied them to her life. She practiced living holy in front of Max, no matter the situation. She listened to gospel music all the time in the truck and in the house. Strangely, Max didn't mind; normally he would go somewhere where he couldn't hear the music or tune it out. She quickly learned if she continued to throw the church in his face, he would develop resentment toward her and the church she attended. After a while, when Sarah and the kids came home from church, he would ask the girls what they learned at church. On Sunday nights, Max sat very engaged while Sarah talked to him about what Bishop Edwards preached at morning service. She wanted to be that light to lead Max out of darkness, and she knew she couldn't be if she allowed her flesh to get in the way. She would share with Max all the things God was doing for her and the blessing he gave her because of her faithfulness to God. Every time she prayed, she asked God to draw Max closer to Him and to show her how to live a holy life in front of him.

She sent Max daily scriptures. Everything she did was like planting a seed into Max's life, and they were watered accordingly. She allowed patience to have its perfect works in her, having no idea the transformation Max was about to undergo.

It was a peaceful day. The night had just taken over daylight. The fresh breeze whistled as it brushed the fragile tree branches in the back yard. The smell from the rain approaching filled the house. Sarah stood in the hall bathroom listening to Mary Mary on the Pandora music app. She was examining her face for any unusual scars, pimples, bags under the eyes, discoloration of the skin or anything that she would need to fix before she graced the world with her presence tomorrow. She heard the phone ring.

"Hello?" answered Max. "Yes, this is Max Houston; how may I help you? Yes, I can be there no later than Tuesday morning. Yes! Thank you, God!" exclaimed Max, shouting loudly, hanging up the phone. Sarah peeked out the bathroom door with curiosity, wondering what the cause of Max's strange behavior was. Max ran to Sarah. He attempted to pick her up in hopes to turn her around in a circle. He put her down and hugged her. "Babe," he said with a big smile on his face. "God is good."

"All the time, and all the time God is good. What's up?"

"God opened the door for me. Can you believe it after sitting unemployed for two and a half months? I was collecting $1,200 in unemployment every two weeks. I was barely making ends meet. I just got a call for a job making $21 an hour, working six tens (six days a week, ten hours a day). Of that, $2.75 will go towards my pension and $100 will go into my annuity. Do you know how much money that is?" Max smiled with gladness. "Oh my God, babe. We will be able to pay all our bills and have money left over." he said with confidence. "How does that sound?" Max looked at Sarah smiling, in hopes that she would smile back. Only if he had known that him getting a job was like a Mississippi Mass Choir who had an overflow of believers in it to tear the roof off the church. Sarah's spirit man sang, "I hear the chains falling," from one of her favorite gospel songs, "Break Every Chain" by Tasha Cobbs. She smiled and gave God a ten second praise dance.

"Wow! God will do exceedingly, abundantly above all we can ask or think. That's amazing! I'm so happy for you!"

"What do you mean happy for me? Be happy for *us*."

Sarah smirked. "So when do you start?"

"I start Tuesday morning. That gives me time to get things together around the house. Oh, but there's one thing," he said frowning.

"What's that?" Sarah stood silent, not having the slightest idea of what he was going to say.

"It's not here. It is in Charleston, South Carolina," he bit the corner of his lip.

"As in out of town, state, region?" She chuckled to hide her disapproval.

"Yes, it's twelve hours away. I have to leave out tomorrow no later than one o'clock that afternoon."

"Wow!" She walked away from Max with her head down. She kicked back her tears and sat down on the black sunken in sofa. Max followed her into the living room. She could hear the swiftness of his feet coming from behind her. He sat down beside her looking sad, putting his arm around her and pulling her close to him. He gently placed her head on his chest.

"Are you going to be okay?" he asked. As she laid on his chest, she could hear his heart beat get louder as a drum in the parade. She felt several thumps from his chest as if his heart had arms and was pushing her away. She recognized his anticipation for her response heighten by the second.

She looked up at Max. "I have no choice." She dropped her head. "It's just that I wasn't prepared for this." She cleared her throat as it became shaky. "I mean, I don't know what to think, how to feel, or anything. Why can't you stay here?" The wells of her eyes filled with tears.

"There's no work here babe. All the work for Ironworkers is backed up in Illinois and St. Louis."

"What about the job you were just working on in East St. Louis? Why can't you go back there? They were paying you $30.35 an hour, along with great benefits."

"The job ended. Unfortunately, the jobs that they have available are given to individuals out of their East Saint Louis local. I've tried so hard to make the hours I needed to transfer over from Atlanta, Georgia local to East Saint Louis or Saint Louis local. But every time I get close, they always have some excuse on why I can't, and I'm tired of it." Max raised his voice.

"When I was working in Saint Louis local, I was making $31.98 an hour with $6.95 going toward pension and $4.30 into my annuity. It seems like when I almost had enough work hours to transfer over, they laid me off. Babe, this is a prejudice business; it's not fair at all." He sighed with disappointment. He shook his head then shrugged his shoulders. "I thank God he gave me everything I needed to pursue my dreams of becoming a Journeyman Ironworker. I am able to go anywhere in the world to work, including Canada and Hawaii. I've worked in Georgia, Mississippi my home state, Florida, Alabama, Memphis, Michigan, Maryland, Louisiana, Illinois, and Missouri. Just know this is only temporary, and I'll be back home before you know it." Max smiled and kissed Sarah on her cheek. Sarah sat in a daze. *Ugh!* She screamed internally. She sighed and began to pray to herself. *Lord, please help me deal with this situation; I'm happy we're going to be able to pay our bills, but I'm sad that he's leaving. Give me a piece of mind and strength to ride this out.* She cleared her throat. "So what now?"

"Well, I have to pack my clothes and work tools, but I'm not going to do anything tonight."

They got off the couch and walked into the bedroom and lay down.

"I'll wait until the morning. I just want to take this time to hold, kiss, and love on you. Now kiss me like you'll never see me again." Max quoted one of his favorite R&B singers Alicia Keys hit single, "Kiss Me like you'll Never See Me Again". Max sang in Sarah's ear while they lay in bed.

"Hey baby doll." Max moved her hair out of her face and kissed her on the forehead. "I just want you close, where you can stay forever." He placed his finger on her chest and began to trace a big heart on it. "You can be sure, that it will only get better." He poked his lip out imitating Sarah and nodded his head, and started singing another Alicia Keys song, "No One". "You and me together," he pointed at her and then himself, "through the days and nights, I don't worry 'cause everything's going to be all right. People keep talking," he held up his left hand and started to make hand gestures as if his hand was talking. "They can say what they like, but all I know is, everything's going to be alright." He gazed into Sarah's eyes so that she would recognize that he meant every word he sang. Sarah turned her back to Max. She closed her eyes and allowed her tears to flow. She took over singing, "when the rain is pouring down, and my heart is hurting. You will always be around, this I know for certain." Sarah became more emotional. She felt her stomach turn over. She could feel every verse she sang. She was suffering at that very moment, and she wasn't sure if Max could make the pain of emptiness go away. Max held her tighter. He kissed her softly on the back of her neck. "Hey, for a second there I thought you were going to leave me singing by myself. That would have been awkward." Max laughed. "If loving you was wrong, I don't want to be right, if being right means being without you I'd rather—

"Max!" Sarah yelled cutting him off from singing. She turned her head slightly. "If you quote another song, I will be forced to tape your mouth shut!"

They both laughed. "Give way to sleep Lil' Daddy. You have a long day ahead of you." They cuddled and closed their eyes and went to bed.

Lowered into a sense of serenity, the silence contained Sarah while the warmth and the glare from the sun met her in the bed from a side window in the sleeping room. Dazed, she smirked as she recalled last night, feeling she could probably lay in bed as free as a bird all day since she was still fragile. She struggled to place her mind and body on the same level. She dreaded having to say goodbye to Max.

"Thank you Lord for this amazing day you have allowed me and my family to partake in," she said softly. Noticing Max's absence, she put on her house slippers and cheetah print silk robe and strutted toward the kitchen.

Mmm, something smells good. I bet I know what it is: pancakes, eggs, rice, sausage and the famous bacon, my baby can't make breakfast without bacon. I would swear up and down he was an undercover spokesman for the Hills Dill Farm or something, she thought. Sarah smiled as she looked at the kitchen table neatly set with a vase filled with pink, white, and red roses from her rose bushes in the front yard. Sitting on the table also were four plates and four cups of Florida Orange Juice with the pulp, her favorite. She looked around, as there was no sign of Max.

"Hey, Baby Doll!" Sarah heard Max's voice penetrate through the back door. He walked into the kitchen, smiling as usual. Sarah's emotional circuits caught fire as he approached her, causing her to blush.

"Hey!" Sarah greeted him with a pleasant kiss. "All this for me?" Sarah smiled. "Now what did I do to deserve such an amazing man? Thank you God," she grinned.

"Baby, this will be the last meal I get to cook for you and the kids before I leave."

"Oh, that's right. Aw!" Sarah poked her lip out as she held back her tears. "I'm going to miss you." Max took a deep breath. "You know I love you. I won't be gone long. I have got to make us some money. I can't just lay around. Man don't work man don't eat, right?"

"Yeah, you're right." Sarah smiled.

"I washed clothes and cleaned up a little. I got the dogs situated. They are securely chained to their dog houses. They won't be able to get out of the yard while you're away from the house. I changed the oil in your truck. That's one less trip you will have to make to the car shop. Now you should be good for a while. At least until I come back home. I don't want you to stress yourself out with any of those things."

Sarah smiled and gave Max a big hug. "Dang, superman, and you managed to cook breakfast too."

"Meanwhile, the girls and work will be the only thing you have to worry about. Although the girls would be the only thing, you have to worry about if you let me bring you off your job. I'll let that be your call, Baby Doll." Max shook his head with disappointment.

Sarah suddenly remembered. "Oh my God, I overslept! What time is it? I'm late for work." Sarah frantically looked around for a clock.

"No you're not," Max started laughing. "I got up early. I figured you would be tired after last night."

"Really!" Sarah smirked.

"Yeah. You know how you be drooling, mouth wide open, snoring." He smiled slightly.

"Well, I guess I'll give it to you and allow you to brag a little this time." She was considerate of his ego. "Probably because you're leaving."

Sarah yelled. "It's time to get up for school." She reminded Haven and Hannah.

The girls joined Max and Sarah shortly after getting dressed for school.

"This is good, thanks, Mom." said Hannah stuffing her face with pancakes.

"Yeah, good," said Haven nodding her head in agreement. She tried imitating Hannah and stuffed her face with pancakes as well.

"Yes, it is good. Daddy cooked." Sarah winked at Max.

"Thanks, Daddy." the girls replied.

Max cooking was no surprise to them since he cooks for them all the time.

"Hey, babe. Time is ticking away from us." Said Max. "Would you like for me to get the children to school?" Max gathered the dishes from off the kitchen table. "No, I'll take them. You relax." Sarah prepared to leave.

Haven and Hannah skipped to the truck while holding their dad's hand.

"Hey Dad," said Hannah. "Are you picking us up from school today?

"No princess. Daddy has to go out of town to work for a while."

"Can I go with you, Daddy? Please?" Hannah poked out her lip, doing what she does best.

"No, not this time, princess," Max was sad, and it showed. "While I'm gone, I want you and Haven to be good and take care of Mom."

"Ok," Haven and Hannah replied together.

"Hey Dad?" Hannah asked. "Why do you have to go out of town and work?"

"Well princess, there's no buildings for me to help build here, but they have some buildings that are being built out of town, and they asked me to help.

"Ok, I love you, Daddy. Be safe. I'll call you when I get out of school."

"I love you too. That would be nice. I'll be waiting to hear from you." Max smiled feeling loved.

Max walked towards Sarah grinning, "I'll see you in a minute, honey." He kissed Sarah on her forehead and stroked her hand.

"I'll be back after I drop the kids off, so I can help you finish packing."

CHAPTER THREE

"I'm really going to miss Daddy when he leaves," Hannah said sadly. "Are you going to miss Daddy when he leaves, Mommy?"

"Of course, honey. Why would you ask me that question?"

"I don't know. I just asked."

"Okay, honey, we're here," Sarah pulled up in front of Hannah's school. "I'll see you later. Make Mommy and Daddy proud today by being a good leader, making the right choices, and most importantly, doing all your work to the best of your ability."

"Okay Mommy, I love you!" She kissed Sarah on her cheek and gave her a gentle hug.

"I love you too, Haven," Hannah kissed her little sister on the forehead and gave her a big hug. Haven squirmed to get away and wiped the kiss off.

Sarah laughed at Hannah and Haven. "You are next, Haven."

"Yes!" Haven grinned from ear to ear.

After dropping Haven off at school, Sarah couldn't help but think about Max leaving. Her phone rang.

"Answer!" Sarah shouted, commanding her phone to accept an incoming call.

Sarah cleared her itchy throat. "Hello?"

"Hey bestie! Has Max left yet?" asked Lauren.

"No, not yet," Sarah cleared her throat.

"What are you doing, crying?" Lauren didn't sound surprised.

"No, I did enough crying last night to last me for a week." Sarah chuckled.

"I know you're going to miss your boo, girl. What are you going to do while he's gone?"

"I can't honestly say that I know. I haven't thought that far ahead. I'm just trying to make it through today."

"How is he getting down there?"

"He's going to drive his truck."

"Did you tell the kids? How are they taking it?"

"They're taking it pretty well, but they really don't understand what's going on," Sarah sighed.

"That makes sense."

"Well, girl I just pulled up in front of our house. I'm going to help him finish packing. I'll talk to you when he leaves."

"Ok, tell him I said drive safe. Make sure you tell him not to be gone for too long. He knows you're scary. You won't be able to stay in the house by yourself for too long. Y'all electric bill is going to be sky high before he gets back. Do you still sleep with every light on in the house when he's not there?"

"Whatever girl. You know I wasn't always like that," Sarah laughed.

"Ok, call me back."

Sarah sat in her truck in front of the house. She began to rationalize after realizing she had mixed feelings about Max leaving.

Should I cry to show him that I'm really going to miss him, or should I keep it together to show him how tough I can be? This will let him know that I'm ready to hold down the house while he's gone. After all, this will be the first time we ever had to be apart from each other since we met three years ago. She stared at a picture of the two of them. "Ugh, man this sucks!" Sarah yelled then got out of the truck.

"Hey Daddy, I'm home. Sarah called out, slamming the door behind her. *You can do this*, she reassured herself. She walked throughout the house, cleaning up a big mess Max made as he packed his things. She walked into their bedroom and flopped down on the edge of the bed. She relentlessly stared into the closet where only her clothes hung now. Reality hit her like a snowplow as Max walked in the room, all dressed to leave. He was leaving much earlier than she anticipated. South Carolina was twelve hours from St Louis. He had to be at work the very next morning. Her heart got tight. Her mouth began to quiver and her eyes began to water.

Oh, here we go, Sarah thought to herself. *I guess I'm going to be a cry baby after all. Oh well.* She let it out; tears filled her lap while her breathing became harder. She could feel that her face was heating up, turning red.

Max rushed over to console her. "Awe baby, it's going to be ok." He wrapped her in his warm cushioned arms.

Sarah's inner tough girl began to speak to her. *Come on girl and stop all that crying! He's coming back. You are acting like he just broke up with you and you just now getting the memo. The sooner he leaves, the sooner he can come back.*

"Are you going to be okay, Momma? Depending on how long I'm going to be gone, you and the kids can come visit me."

Max knew Sarah had no problem jumping on the highway to travel out of town.

"I'm just worried. Where are you going to stay so you can sleep?"

"You know me--I'll sleep in my truck until I can't afford a hotel room. I survived hurricane Katrina remember? I was sitting in my car on the side of the road for three days. I have just enough money to get me down there. I packed enough food to hold me over 'til the beginning of next week. A good friend of mine is going to wire me $100 until I get my first check."

Sarah felt a little better knowing he had a Trailblazer and the back seats breakdown. Sarah walked Max to the truck with her arms wrapped tightly around his waist. She hoped he would get a call from his BA (Business Agent) in any minute to let him know that they found a job closer to home so he didn't have to go to South Carolina. So much for wishful thinking. Max got into the truck and cranked it. Determined and anxious, Sarah stood on the truck lift and reached into the window. She wrapped her arms around his neck, refusing to let go. With an anticipation on the rise she didn't give much thought to her surroundings, not to mention her actions. She swung the truck door open with self-seeking intentions.

"Hey baby," Max said kissing Sarah on her cheek. "I have

to get going before it gets too late."

"Ok, Lil' Daddy." Sarah stepped down from the truck lift.

Max pulled out of the driveway. He blew her a kiss. His Live to Inspire cologne lingered, as well as the thoughts she created. Her thoughts held her captive, overwhelming and satisfying her mentally. She wished it was everything but a mild fantasy. However, she didn't want Max to be sleepy while driving.

"I'm going to miss my Lil' Daddy." Sarah poked her lip out.

She went back into the house and finished cleaning up. She wanted to hold on to her current thoughts of Max a little while longer, so she called into work to inform her boss she wasn't coming in. Her eyes grew hefty as she sat on the couch, reading over a text message Max sent her.

Incoherent, Sarah texted, "lkljihuh." Her hands lost mobility and her phone fell onto the floor. Her body shut down from sobbing, and she cried herself into a much-needed nap.

"Honey, I'm home." Max dropped his bags in the middle of the floor. The aroma of last night's leftovers seeped through the microwave oven. "Hmm, something smells good Momma," Max broadcasted. He looked around waiting for a reply. The house was silent. There wasn't a soul in sight. Max walked over trash and toys as he investigated every room in the household in hopes to see someone, but he was not successful until he saw steam coming from underneath the bathroom door. He lay across the bed and dozed off.

The bathroom door opened a little while later, releasing a sufficient amount of steam that pressed its way into the bedroom where Max laid sleep from exhaustion. He was awakened by a soft snicker and a gentle touch. A beautiful smile captivated him while alluring eyes embraced his presence. Feeling privileged, Max addressed the woman by the nickname he created for her. He gave her a sentimental kiss.

"Hey, I've missed you so much." The woman smiled as her heart sang with gladness. "Why you didn't call and let me know you were coming home?"

"So, I have to check in before I come home now?"

"No babe, I'm saying, I would have went shopping and bought the things you like, and of course cleaned up." She pushed the clothes to the already crowded floor. She was embarrassed that she hadn't cleaned her bedroom.

"No, you're all right; I'm not going to be here long." Max reached for his phone as he laid on the bed. "This job is only for four weeks."

"Oh ok. I know what we're going to be doing every day until you leave." The woman was ecstatic.

"Where's the little man?"

"He's at school. I know he is going to be happy to see his daddy. Will you be going with me to pick him up?"

"Of course! That would be great," Max looked at his phone to check the time once more.

Ten minutes before dismissal they arrived at their two-year-old's school. Max went into the main office and signed Alex out before picking him up from his classroom.

"Hey, Lil man," Max whispered into his son's ear as he listened to his teacher give instructions for dismissal.

"Daddy, Daddy, this my daddy!" his son screamed. "Hey everybody, say hi to my daddy!" Alex hugged his dad tightly. Alex's mother leaned on the door smiling at them. She was trying not to cry.

They got into the car.

"Where to now?" Alex mom asked.

Alex shouted. "Home! I want to play with my daddy." Alex smiled brightly.

"It's crazy how two years can go by so fast. I just realized that we haven't seen each other since I became pregnant with Alex. We talked on the phone, but since we were able to video chat every day, it seems like you never left," She smiled rubbing Max's leg.

A loud, annoying sound repeatedly echoed in Sarah's ear. She jumped up from her dream and shut off her alarm clock she set reminding her to go pick up Haven and Hannah from school. She collected her thoughts, leaving the ones she didn't have the desire to take along with her where she generated them. She sprinted out the door.

After picking up the girls from school, Sarah went over to her mother's house so the girls could see their grandmother and also to pass the time. Sarah's sister, Evans, stopped by to see Hannah and Haven before they went home.

"Hey sis! What's up? Mom told me that Max got a job out of town. Will you be alright at the house without him?" Evans asked.

"The girls and I will be ok. Thanks for asking," Sarah smiled.

"Do you remember that day I came over to your house?"

"No! When don't you come over?" Sarah asked playfully.

Evans laughed, "You know, when you and Max had that argument."

Feeling bothered, Sarah placed her feet on the foot stool in front of her. She rocked continually in the rocking chair as she reminisced on that unforgettable day.

"That was crazy," Sarah laughed off her discomfort, looking at Evans. "Why did you ask me about that night?" Sarah couldn't help but wonder what she would say.

"I have to tell you what happen that night I went out." Evans looked as if she had something good and juicy to tell Sarah.

"No." Sarah's flesh wanted to know badly and couldn't wait to hear it. However, her spirit man said, "*You should tell her that you don't want to know. You know how messy she can be with gossip.*"

Battling between her flesh and spirit man, Sarah foolishly gave into her flesh.

"Girl!" Evans said long and ghetto, smacking her lips.

Sarah hates when she does that. She squinted her eyes and looked at her as she regained her hearing.

"Do you remember my friend Tasha?" Evans asked.

"Yes, the one that's married to her cousin's ex-husband, Jimmy, right?"

"Yes girl. Wait, how did you know that?" Evans looked surprised.

"Uh, because you told me of course. You forgot. You know, you tell me everything and you tell everybody's business. Don't let me find out you be telling my business to your nosey friends and your momma. That will be the last story you tell before you come up missing." Sarah gave her a mean mug.

"Girl no, that's like suicide. I would never do you like that." She seemed she would tell something top secret if the price was right.

"Ok, let me tell you. She— wait, where is Momma?" Evans cautiously looked around for her.

"She is upstairs with Hannah and Haven. Why did you ask?"

"Girl, you know Momma is as nosey as heck. By the time I finish telling you, she would have told five people what I'm about to tell you."

"True. You're right about that. That's your momma." Sarah laughed.

"Anyways, for the last six months Tasha's husband had taken a couple of business trips. More than she anticipated this time around. She had a bad feeling something wasn't right." Evans explained.

"Oh, wow." Sarah couldn't help but feel sad for Tasha. She knew firsthand how she could have felt. Sarah shook her head. She felt guilty for listening to Evan's gossip about her friend, but it was too late to stop her from talking. Sarah was already heavily engaged into the conversation. Her ears were itching for more. Sarah sat silently and insisted Evans finish telling her what happen. As she listened to Evans finish her story, she was doubtful, confused, disgusted, and was reassured of why she thought Evans was crazy as hail stones in the summer time.

"Girl, you are your mother's child," Sarah said, getting up from the table. "Well, it's been fun, sis, and very interesting. Hannah, Haven, and I are going to head home. It's been a long day, and I just want this day to be over with already."

"I hear you sis." Evans got up and gave Sarah a long hug. She knew she was already missing Max and that it may be hard for her to get any sleep tonight.

"Ugh!" Sarah screamed.

"Ok, what was that about?" Evans asked, looking puzzled.

"I have to un-filter that mess you told me about Tasha and her husband. Knowing that Max is so far away, I don't want to think that Max is doing the same thing Jimmy did. I'll be calling that man accusing him of cheating on me. That's not even my character. That's exactly why I watch what goes into my eye and ear gate. Evil communication corrupts good manners."

Evans rolled her eyes. "I love you. Drive safe. Hey, make sure you turn those dang gone lights off in the house when you go to sleep. Max is going to go crazy if he comes home to a high electric bill."

"Shut up! Don't judge me. I have to see what's going on in the house the entire time. I love you more."

CHAPTER FOUR

It's been a month since Max had been gone, but oftentimes, Sarah felt he had just left. She continued to text Max daily scriptures along with prayers of covering and wisdom while he was on the job. Sarah started noticing a remarkable change in Max while he was away. He would call thanking Sarah for the scriptures that she texted him. Although she couldn't always talk to him about the Bible, that didn't stop her from slowly revealing the Bible to him through words of encouragement based off God's word. She didn't have a chance to talk to Max as much as she'd hope because he read his Bible on his lunch break. She wouldn't have dared to interrupt his time with God. She knew that his dedication and commitment to God would reflect his dedication and commitment to her as his wife. It states in the bible, "Surely, wherever your treasure is, there your heart will also be."

Besides going to church on Sundays, Bible study on Wednesday, outreach twice every two weeks, prayer every other Friday night-- Hannah's dance rehearsals and work kept Sarah busy. Consequently, she didn't think about Max as much as she would have loved to. Sarah believed that's what God wanted. He wanted her to draw near to him. A unmarried woman or virgin is concerned about the Lord's affairs. Her aim was to be devoted to the Lord in both body and spirit. Max's absence limited their chances of fornication. Bishop Edwards told Sarah that it's impossible for a man and woman to stay in the same house and not be intimate. As long as Max was around, she couldn't give God her full focus. She was concerned with Max's affairs and how she could please him.

Max headed home after being gone for seven weeks. Sarah's phone rang. She answered on the first ring. "Hey baby.

How are you? You just don't know how much I've missed you. When are you coming home?"

"Hold on," Max said, putting Sarah on hold. "Hey baby, I'm back. Do you remember a good friend of mine I was telling you about? He stays in St. Louis."

"No, not really. You have a lot of friends, so I lost count."

"He is a first-year apprentice. When we worked together, we shared a hotel room. You know it's not too many people I would be willing to share a room with."

"Oh yeah." Sarah still wasn't sure who he was. "What's his name again?"

"Derrick Mane. So, what are you doing?"

"Waiting on you to tell me when you're coming home."

Max laughed. "When do you want me to come home?"

"Uh, like yesterday." Sarah giggled.

"Derrick rode with me from South Carolina. I'm going to stop by the house and drop my things off, then drop Derrick off at home is that okay with you, baby doll."

"What! You're here, in St. Louis, and you didn't tell me!?"

"Well, babe, I wanted to surprise you. I'm about an hour away."

"Ok, sounds good. Let me jump in the shower." Sarah started the shower than ran into the basement for a face towel.

She rushed into the bathroom and took a quick shower. She wasn't sure how far away Max was since he didn't tell her he was coming home so soon. She put on her clothes and walked out the bathroom.

Max laid across the bed smiling. He called Sarah's phone. Sarah heard her phone ring and ran to the bedroom to get it.

"Jesus!" She yelled as she opened the bedroom door. Max smiled.

"Why would you do that?" She hit Max repeatedly in his chest. It took her full focus to preserve her heart from exploding out of her chest.

Max quickly grabbed Sarah and pulled her close to him. He hugged her tight and kissed her gently on her forehead. "I miss you." He smiled.

"When did you get here?"

"I was already outside the house when you told me you were going to take a shower."

"Where is your friend, Derrick?"

"He's in the truck waiting on me. I told him to give me a minute because I had an overdue package I had to deliver to you. I explained to him that I couldn't drop it off. You had to sign for it." Max just smiled.

"Wow, shut up. You did not tell him that. Although I wouldn't be surprised if you did."

"Don't worry, I didn't tell him that." He smirked, looking very suspicious. "Baby Doll, can you do me a favor?"

"Sure, anything for you Lil Daddy."

"Please, please put some different clothes on before you get both of us in trouble. I'm not trying to be on God's wall of shame for fornicating. Let's keep it holy. Even though, I almost made you lay your Holy Spirit to the side. I know you wanted to curse after I scared you."

"Ok." Sarah smiled. She went into the closet and put on the first thing she saw.

After Sarah changed clothes, she and Max walked into the front room. He opened the front door and called out for Derrick to come into the house.

"Hey baby, come meet Derrick," Max yelled.

Sarah gradually made her way to join Max. Derrick was looking out of the window onto the yard. He smiled as Sarah approached him. He could see her reflection from the window.

"This is the person you're talking about!?" Sarah blurted out. She was surprised. She took a quick glance in the mirror that hung behind her.

"Yes, baby doll. Why did you say it like that?"

"Because I didn't know you were talking about him. Had I known it was him, I would have put on something different." Sarah adjusted Max's worn tank top and black loosely fitted jogging pants she was wearing.

Max looked confused.

Derrick turned around smiling. "Well, look at what we have

here. Sarah, Sarah. Hmm, still looking good I see." Derrick shook his head.

"Man, where have you been? I have been looking for you nonstop. Jack and I were just talking about you yesterday. We were talking about how you were always fun to be around. I have the night we kicked it preserved in my long term memory. You wore that orange—

"Boy, stop it." Sarah responded in a tone Max consider to be playful and flirty.

Max stepped back from in front of Sarah and turned towards Derrick. Max stared at him as if he was a lion awaiting his prey.

"It's been a very long time since I've seen you. You still look the same. Imagine that," said Derrick.

Sarah smiled back and blushed.

Max had an instant adrenaline rush while hoping to stay in control of his anger. Although Max was furious at the both of them, he stood in silence, not wanting to miss any indication that Derrick and Sarah had been together physically.

"Get over here, girl, and give me a hug," Derrick shouted. He held his arms out inviting Sarah into his personal space.

She ran over to Derrick giving him a long, soothing hug. She raised her right leg from off the floor as he picked her up, turning her around in a full circle. "Oh, how I missed you," Derrick said, removing his arms from around Sarah, overlooking Max mean mugging him.

Max stood in silence, looking at Derrick as if he had stolen his trophy after a long competitive competition.

"Hey babe, why are you looking like that?" Sarah kissed Max on the cheek.

"Will somebody tell me what's going on here? Explain to me why my woman and close friend standing in front of me with their hands all over each other like this?"

"Baby, I know him. We go way back, oh my God!" Sarah became excited.

"Derrick, I have been thinking about you also." She smiled at him.

"We go way back, don't we?" Derrick asked, and she grinned and nodded her head in a slow motion.

"Yes, way back," Sarah agreed with a smile.

"Way back like how?" Max said awaiting an explanation.

"Man, let me clear this up." Derrick tried to explain.

"No, Let me," Sarah said, cutting Derrick off from talking. "I'm sure he doesn't want to hear it from you. Trust me." She tilted her head slightly and raised her right eyebrow.

"We never did anything. He's like my big brother. He was always there for me. I didn't have anyone to turn to when I felt down and out, so I turned to him. I never had to worry about him judging me for the many things I had done."

"Right, and you were always there for me too, lil sis," Derrick said nodding his head. "He use to talk to my sister, Evans. Come here, let me show you."

Sarah pulled out her phone to log onto her Facebook page. She scrolled through her pictures. "Take a look. Here are Derrick and Evans at a dinner. Here they are at the beach, and here they are again the night Derrick apparently made a mistake by proposing to Evans." Sarah chuckled.

"Yeah man. I just knew she was the one. I guess I was wrong." Derrick said shaking his head.

"Yes, if I had known that I would have told you that wasn't going to work out. Evans is a man devourer. I've seen her woo guys and bury them all in the same sentence, less than a minute." Max said, laughing.

Max felt a sense of relief knowing that Derrick and Sarah had never been close and personal or dated.

Sarah had a lot of love for Derrick, but she had always disliked his approach when it came to women. She describes him as being a Mount Rushmore, a sucker for love who rushed into relationships, putting every woman he met on a mountain of royalty. You know the guy that swears he's head over hills in love with a girl, and they just met a week ago. He's out looking at engagement rings in hopes she would say 'I do' after their fifth date of dating for a month. He's just looking for someone to love him as much as he knows he can love them.

Sarah wrapped her arms around Max and kissed him all over his face. "You know I love you, right?" Sarah stared into Max's eyes. Max smiled, holding on to Sarah as if his life depended on it.

CHAPTER FIVE

"Well, now that we have established that, I don't have to put you in a coma for hugging on my future wife. Have a seat, man." Max said favorably. "I see you guys have some catching up to do. I'll let you guys talk while I get my things from out of the truck. When I finish, I'll be ready to drop you off, man," Max walked outdoors, leaving the screen door to close by itself behind him.

Derrick sat down on the couch and looked at Sarah. "So my man Max is the reason everybody saying you changed and don't kick it like you use to?" asked Derrick. "That's great and all, but I want to know what your intentions towards Max are." Derrick said as he stroked his goatee. "Max and I have been friends for some years now. There is a friend who sticks closer than a brother. That's Max."

"That's true." Sarah agreed nodding her head.

"He has done more for me since I've known him; whereas my family wouldn't, and they have known me all my life. I can count on him to help me when most people turns their back on me even after I helped them."

"Yeah that's one of the many things I love about him." said Sarah. She sat down at the kitchen table.

"I'm looking out for my man's best interest— as a friend, that is. I know he's a good dude. I also know what kind of money he makes, so I just want to know, are you serious about being with him or is this only temporary like your seasonal flings?" Derrick stared at Sarah as she chuckled. "Before you say anything, remember we use to kick it. You use to tell me everything."

Sarah laughed. "No, it's crazy because some time ago, I wouldn't never have taken Max seriously. He was nothing like I wanted, but he was everything I needed to transform my life for the better. You know how I felt about settling down. I wasn't fond of getting married because all the married people I knew were committed to cheating on their spouse. I didn't want that. I didn't want a man to call my own. I just wanted one when I needed a quick fix, minus the obligations that would weigh heavily over my head. The sex I often engaged in fell short of what I expected, wasting my time and energy leaving me empty, yucky, and still hungry. The guys I had relations with agreed to a sex driven relationship. That meant no cuddling, no long conversations over the phone, or texts filled with emotions. I have to admit that living a life of sin don't come cheap; it's filled with dangerous people and life-changing diseases. I thank God I never had to make a trip to the clinic. I remember my sixth-grade teacher said something that stuck with me for years, and I have found with my experience with men. Her theory holds a lot of weight. 'If a man does not love a woman, he will never love that woman, but if a woman doesn't love a man over time she will grow to love him'."

"Yeah, that's about right," Derrick nodded his head in agreement.

"That's what happen between Max and me. Before I met Max, I was fed-up with messing around with these fun boys that proclaimed to be real men. I remember making a covenant with my eyes. I would never look at a man again with the intention of sleeping with him. I promised myself that Hannah would be my primary focus along with work and purchasing a house at the age of 21. Then out of thin air, Max came along to assist us along the way. I would have never thought we would be where we are now, being I wasn't trying to be with him or anyone else at the time."

"That's great, man; he's a good dude. Yeah, that theory does hold a lot of weight, and you would know, you been messing around with grown men since you were nine years old."

"Shut up, Derrick," Sarah said laughing, "No, I started at 14."

"Yeah, I remember you were tricking them old men out their money. Those fools were old enough to be your daddy."

"I know, right? It was funny then, but not so much now. I

allowed the money, cars, and clothes to pull me out of childhood. The guys I talked to had already lived their life as teens, but they didn't care about me living mine. They gave me things I desired to have that my parents couldn't afford to buy me."

Sarah shook her head. "It all came at a price. It became a large bill that was due to be cashed. When I was old enough-- or should I say willing enough-- to have sex with them, the things they bought me, the money they gave and the cars they allowed me to drive increased drastically. What will it profit a man to gain the whole world, but lose his soul?"

Derrick shook his head. "I remember when that guy bought you a pair of Jordan's and your big brother Jimmy found them." Derrick laughed.

"Yes," Sarah said laughing along with him. "I remember I tried to lie about it too."

"That's funny. Now I am almost certain you got your player skills from your brother. Do you think he knew you were lying?"

"Yep, but at that point in the game, there was nothing he could really do or say. I had gone to great lengths to lie to him about the shoes. Who knew what else I would lie about? I've learned that lying is like any addiction. If you don't stop doing it, it becomes harmful, damaging functional traits you preserve like honesty; it can also destroy close relationships that would require years of forgiveness to repair. You would better off be a poor man than a liar. He should have taken the time to teach me the pros and cons of the dating game instead of sheltering me from it. I would have been more open to talking to him about some of the things I was sneaking around doing. I learned how to get what I wanted from guys by watching him manipulate women. I always wondered how it was possible for him to make time for all of those women he talked to. Most of them knew about each other. That was crazy to me."

Derrick shook his head. "But it seems like you've changed for the better."

"I'm not happy about my past, yet I'm not ashamed.

When I established a relationship with Christ, I saw that He didn't approve of adultery, lust, and fornication and that marriage between a man and woman is pleasing in his eyes. I refrained from my old lifestyle.

"That's good, man." Derrick grinned. "God is amazing. So are you guys going to get married?"

"I can happily say yes. I love me some him; he treats me so well. Trust, it wasn't long before I found out what kind of money he made, but that has never been a factor. I was with him when he didn't have any money, and I held him down, but that's another story. I'd rather not go into that. Just know it's not about the money." Sarah giggled. "Plus, I wouldn't last a day in today's dating society. They are just too crazy and open for me, if you know what I mean. I ran into an old friend of mine named Brandy at a church convention. She shared a touching story with me; it just made me thankful for God sending Max into my life to slow me down."

Sarah continued. "Her testimony was amazing, and it had God written all over it. Sarah shared her friend's story with Derrick.

"That's a nice ministry." Derrick said. "People get treated badly because they don't demand respect. I'm not talking about in a harsh way, but based on how they allow other people to treat them. The things they say and do around them and to them. All a man needs is one time to disrespect a woman. If she doesn't correct it, instead she accepts it, she will open a floodgate for more attacks, whether it be emotional, mental, physical or spiritual, but you already know that." Derrick smiled at Sarah.

"What I miss?" Max said, walking into the house with his luggage.

Sarah blew Max a kiss as he came through the door. "Nothing. I was telling Derrick about Brandy. What are you doing outside? It's taking you forever to bring your bags in."

"I just started taking them out my truck. I stopped to talk to our neighbors. I didn't want to rush you and Derrick. Are you ready man?" Max asked Derrick before going back outside to get the rest of his luggage.

"Yeah." Derrick stood up. "Well Sarah, it was nice catching up with you."

"Ok," Sarah stood up. "You got a word for me, prophet?"

"Yes! God said stop looking for every prophet you meet to speak into your life, especially when God has already told you what to do in the situation. God said silence the voices around you as well as the one within you. The more you yield to the Holy Spirit, the less likely you are to stumble. He said don't worry about Max. You and him are going to be fine. God said stop doubting yourself. There have been times that He's told you to do something, and you weren't sure if it was him telling you to do it."

"Yes." Sarah mumbled.

"He said it was Him, and He still wants you to do it. Stop overthinking things. Max is going to get a financial blessing, and you are going to reap the benefits." Derrick concluded.

Sarah looked up at the ceiling, "I hear you God. The Bible states you believe in my prophet so shall you prosper. I believe and receive that prophetic word. I needed to hear that word from God. Thanks," Sarah smiled.

"See you later sis," said Derrick. Sarah hugged Derrick before he walked out the door.

"Ok baby," Max said, putting his luggage in the house. "I'll see you in a minute; I love you much." Max kissed Sarah on her cheek.

CHAPTER SIX

Max was home after being away for seven weeks. As bad as Sarah wanted to, she couldn't be intimate with him. Even though they slipped up before he left to go out of town. He was home again, but this time he had established a relationship with God. He was praying before he went to sleep. He read his Bible daily: morning, noon and night— more than Sarah, actually. Sarah wanted Max even more as she witnessed him becoming closer to God. Sarah's temptation for Max heightened, putting her at risk of grieving the Holy Spirit and fulfilling her fleshly desires. However, this time around, Max was stronger than Sarah in that area, so they were able to keep from fornicating.

Max got a job working about one hour from the house. He was scheduled to work six days, 10 hour shifts a week, but due to the constant rainouts followed by safety concerns, his hours were limited. He got word that his two uncles whom he was very close to, followed by his grandmother who practically raised him had passed. In the midst of his life being turned upside down, he still came to church with no drawbacks. However, the one thing Sarah desired him to get, he didn't. It seemed God's spirit (Holy Spirit) was unfeasible when it came to Max. Sarah talked with Bishop Edwards, voicing her concerns about Max not receiving the Holy Spirit. He told her it could be that Max doesn't believe. She could attest to that because he laughed at her when she told him she had received it. He said the church taught her to speak in tongues. He said it could also be that he's hoarding un-forgiveness in his heart. Sarah thought about his past relationships and things he had shared with her. She deduced that his past was seriously blocking their future, making it impossible for them to accomplish anything together. Sarah admitted at times she wanted to throw in the towel because his burdens were too much for her to bear; she refused to sacrifice her sanity. Max was not willing to cast his cares on the Lord; he felt like there was nothing he couldn't fix himself. Every Sunday, Sarah wanted Max to go down during the altar call, now more than ever before due to everything that was going on in his life. She knew him getting filled with the Holy Spirit would help him, but he didn't think so. He figured surrendering to God and coming to church every Sunday was good enough. She began to feel like she and Max getting married and living holy together was entirely a joke.

Sarah was feeling down. *Maybe we weren't meant to be together forever,* she thought with a deep sigh.

Sarah told Max she couldn't be with him any longer. He wasn't trying hard enough to receive the Holy Spirit. She felt he was holding them back from receiving everything God had for them.

Max got very upset, but he didn't say or do anything. He looked at her with hurt in his eyes.

Sarah felt relieved but only for a moment. Max packed all his things and left. There was no staying in the basement this time, more so because he had the money to get a place elsewhere. Max texted Sarah later that night and informed her that he was headed to Mississippi to work because he knew the weather would be beautiful. He didn't have to worry about going home early due to the rain.

Sarah replied "Ok." As bad as she wanted to say, "No baby, come back home. I'm sorry," she didn't. She believed that if God brought her to it, then He was going to bring her through it.

Sarah had some good days and some bad days while Max was gone. She couldn't believe she broke up with him. Her nights seemed long as she tossed and turned and oftentimes reached out for Max and her days weren't long enough. She spent most of that time looking down at he phone hoping for a text from Max, him asking her how her day is going and telling her I can't wait to see her. She would cook, and out of habit, make Max a plate as if he would walk through the door at any given time. She sat outside in the afternoon as she always did watching everyone in the neighborhood. She envisioned Max pulling up into the drive way after a long day of work like he use to do. He would be smiling, happy to see Sarah and the girls. She tried living her life without him, yet it seemed impossible to get over his warm hugs and late night kisses. She missed falling to sleep on his chest as they watched movies.

Weeks had passed. Sarah called Max as she did every day since they broke up.

"Hey, how are you doing today?" Sarah asked Max.

"I'm okay. How are you and the girls?"

"They keep asking about you, wondering when they're going to be able to see you. I told them you were working."

"Ok, do you mind answering this question for me?"

"Go ahead. I'm all ears."

"Why do you keep calling me, after you said you didn't want to be with me anymore?"

Sarah's heart stopped. "Well, I don't hate you. I still love you. We have kids together. Who else is going to check on you other than me?"

"I can't take it. For me to know that I'm not with you, and I never will be again. Or should I say, to know what it's like to have you in my life, and then have to continue life without you, hearing your voice every day is not helping either. I promise, I don't want to hate you for the decision you made to push me out of your life."

"I'm sorry. I won't call you as much. I didn't know you felt that way. When are you coming to see our kids?"

"I will have to see. This job is about to end in three days. A job called me to work in Granite City, Illinois for three weeks, so I'll be headed that way shortly. I'll just have to find a hotel where the girls can come visit me."

"The hotel? Really! You said you didn't hate me. That's like torture if you take the girls to a hotel so that you can spend time with them. We have a house with a backyard; there's no need for you to go to a hotel. You do still pay bills here. Therefore, you can stay at the house. I haven't replaced you with anyone."

"Ok, I have to get back to work talk to you later."

"Ok, I love you. Sorry, sorry," Sarah chuckled before hanging up the phone."

Max arrived at their house as he had promised three days later. The kids heard the screen door open, and ran to the front of the house screaming with excitement. They peeped out the window next to the door and saw that it was Max.

"Mom, it's Daddy! It's Daddy!" the girls yelled at the same time.

Sarah gave them permission to open the door. Max was halfway through the door when the girls jumped on him with eagerness, forcing him to the floor.

"We missed you!" Hannah said, smiling from ear to ear.

Sarah stood back, smiling at them. Seeing Max was unreal and hard for Sarah. She walked in the other room to cry.

"Oh, how I missed him so much," Sarah mumbled.

She thought back on the 32 days she went to sleep crying and woke up crying, wishing he was there with her and the girls. After he had got the girls settled, Sarah, Max, Hannah, and Haven sat down on the couch and watched movies. By the second movie, the girls were sleeping, and so was Max. Sarah took the girls and put them in their beds. She covered Max with a blanket, kissing him on his lips.

"Why did I do that?" Sarah thought to herself. "Oh, Lord." Sarah rushed to her bedroom and went to bed before a kiss wasn't the only thing she was going to take from Max.

Sarah and the girls prepared for church. Sarah was uncertain about Max's thoughts of joining them at church, so she did not ask. Later, Max got dressed for church. He asked Sarah if he should wear a blue or black shirt. Before Sarah could respond, she had a glimpse of something it hit her like an explosive.

He's going to get filled with God's spirit today, Sarah thought to herself. She quickly remembered a vision she had a while back. Max was wearing a black shirt when he became saved. They took him to the upper room. He later walked up to Sarah after coming from the upper room and said he received the Holy Spirit.

"The black one." said Sarah. Sarah stared at him in a daze while Max put on his clothes.

"What's wrong Sarah?" Max asked. "You thought I wasn't going to church."

"No, I didn't think anything."

"You don't have to sit with me if you don't want to." Max responded feeling uneasy.

"Really. I have no problem with you sitting with me, plus it would be weird for the girls if you didn't," said Sarah.

During church service, Sarah felt different. It was a feeling she had never felt before. She was anticipating altar call, and she feared it wasn't coming soon enough. Once Bishop Edwards finished his sermon, an elder initiated altar call. Sarah prayed in the spirit, as she always does during the altar call. She learned that doing so would help keep away any demonic spirits from entering her if one were to be cast out of someone else and also to pray for individuals to get saved. Sarah wanted to open her eyes to see if Max had gone down to the altar, but the Holy Spirit told her to keep her eyes closed and not to worry about Max. Less than a minute, she felt a tug on her leg, followed by cheering. When she opened her eyes, she saw Haven holding onto her leg. She picked her up and browsed for Max. He had gone down to meet the elders. The elders took him to a secluded room located in the back of the church.

A half an hour had passed. Sarah was fellowshipping with her brothers and sisters in Christ when a deacon came up to her smiling. "God filled Max. I am happy for him. The first thing came to mind was, 'I bet Sarah's happy'." The deacon was overjoyed.

"Praise God! That's good news!" Sarah and everyone that

was standing with her rejoiced.

Sarah waited around the sanctuary for Max to return. She wanted to kiss and hug on him, but she couldn't because they were no longer together. Sarah was afraid she had lost him forever since they had never voided their relationship. One would say that she manipulated him into wanting God's spirit. She became alarmed when she thought about something Bishop Edwards preached. He said what if the man you brought to Christ to get saved wasn't the man God wanted you to marry? What if your job was to get him saved and he was to later marry someone else?

Max walked up to Sarah and tapped her on the shoulder. Sarah turned around and smiled. She waited for Max to say something as she observed his light pink eyes and heavenly glow, but Max just stood there speechless, nodding and smiling as everyone congratulated him on receiving the Holy Spirit. Sarah gathered the girls and headed to the truck. The ride home was mute. There was not much said over dinner neither. Max put the girls to bed.

Sarah and Max sat in the backyard and talked for the first time in a while.

Sarah cleared her throat and spoke softly. "So, how do you feel?"

"I feel like a weight has been lifted off my shoulders."

"I felt the same way when God filled me."

They stayed up for hours talking. It was clear that their lives wouldn't be the same without each other, so they reactivated their relationship and agreed to allow God to work on them individually so that they may be perfect for one another. This did not come without a challenge for Sarah. Max paid for Sarah to go to school to be a Nail Tech. Once she passed her State Board Examinations, she worked in a few salons. A friend of hers referred her to a Salon where she worked. The friend said she was looking for a nail technician. Sarah went to an interview and got hired on the spot.

Sarah ministered to a lot of people while she worked at the

salon. She would even invite them out to her church. Many came and went, but one particular client stuck around. He came to church faithfully every Sunday after he left his church. He was his church's musician. Sarah's church had a prayer line, so every morning, saints would gather on the line and pray for an hour. The pastor conducting prayer line would allow everyone to submit a prayer request. Sarah's faithful client got on the line every day and his request would be the same.

"I would like to pray for Sarah. Also I desire to have a wife I want God to send me a wife. Thank you." said Sarah's client.

Sarah was happy that he was leaning towards God. At her job, she was sitting in hot water. It seemed everyone who once thought she was a blessing to the salon, and everyone who came to her for Godly advice started treating her badly. They said she was too zealous about God. They quoted scriptures to try and justify their behavior towards her. They start talking about things in front of her that they know she didn't stand for. They did everything to make her upset to see if she was as saved as she proclaimed to be. Every time she got ready to quit, she was reminded of what one of her clients said. She told Sarah that she was on assignment by God. She told her the assignment will be over after fourteen months. So Sarah stuck it out, but the closer it got to the date, it became hard for Sarah to hang in there. During the fourteenth month of her assignment, she sat in her car every day in the morning before work and prayed to God, asking him to help her through this until the end. She had a lot going on in her life at that time.

A relative had passed, and she was asked to give a scripture reading. The funeral was on a Friday, which was a busy work day for Sarah at the salon. She also was in her best friend's wedding the following week.

Sarah sat in her truck outside of work contemplating if she was going to go in.

"Lord, I know you said this would be the month that my assignment is over. I'm trying my best to be patient, but these people are going to make me lose my tongue, and I'm afraid I'll lose whatever witness I may have had. Lord, whenever you decide to remove me from this place, please make it clear so that I can understand because you know I don't always get when you tell me things. You have to show me. Make it so plain a child could figure it out." Sarah got out of her truck and went into the salon with a sense of peace.

She stopped at the front desk to inform the secretary of the days she would not be able to work and the reason why. She told her client to follow her back to her work area. While Sarah was doing her client's pedicure, her boss's assistant approached her.

"Hey, Sarah I see you put in all these days to be absent and that's not acceptable. The salon is very busy on those days. You can't take off for a funeral if the person is not your parent or sibling. Do you want to take a temporary leave of absence and just come back when you're ready to be committed to the salon? Meanwhile we will find someone to fill your position."

"That's fine." Sarah tended to her client. She could hear her boss and his assistant discussing Sarah.

Her boss assistant walked back over to Sarah. She put her hands in her pocket and stood beside Sarah. "Sarah, he said we can't afford to let you take leave, so we have to let you go. Do we owe you anything?"

"No."

"So once you're finished with your client, you can get your things and leave."

"Ok." Sarah continued working on her client. Sarah smiled.

"Thank you, God." Sarah mumbled.

"Oh my God, are you ok? I can't believe she would fire you in front of me like that. I've never seen them do such a thing as this before, and I've been coming here for years. How are you going to get money? Don't you have kids? You don't seem bothered by this. You don't have to finish my nails."

"I have never felt better. I will be alright. God supplies all my needs. My prayers have been answered. I'm going to finish your nails because I've already started."

Sarah finish her client's nails. Her client gave her a thirty dollar tip. Sarah gathered her things, and the secretary handed Sarah her Nail Tech license from off the wall. Sarah walked over to her boss and his assistant and thanked them for the job opportunity.

Max called Sarah from work.

"Hey babe!" Max said.

"Hey, how's it going?"

"Babe, guess who called me!"

"Saint Louis!" Sarah became happy.

"No, although that would have been nice. Someone from the union hall in New York City!" Max shouted with excitement.

"Wow! Are you serious?" Sarah was just as happy as Max. "Go God."

"Yes, thank God. It has always been a dream of mine to work in New York; it's one of the highest paid states in Ironworkers industry. I'm so excited."

"When do you leave?"

"They said I have to be there Tuesday morning for orientation."

"Wow, how are you going to get there? I know you don't like planes."

"I'm going to drive. I'll tell you more about it when I get off work. I couldn't concentrate after they called. All I could think about is telling you the good news, so I came into the porter john to call you. I have to get back to work. I love you."

"Ok, see you soon. I love you too." Sarah hung up the phone. "Thank you God!" Sarah kicked her feet up in a cycling motion. She jumped to her feet and danced, praising God. Derrick's prophecy had come to pass. While waiting for Max to arrive home from work, Sarah thought about the conversation she had with Max's friend Amy when they visited her in Michigan two years ago.

"Hey, my name is Amy. Max has told me so much about you." She approached Sarah with a hug. "Max has told me you guys are getting married," Amy smiled.

"Yes, we are." Sarah smiled back.

"I married a traveling Ironworker. I'm sure you have heard of Corey," Amy said, awaiting Sarah's response.

"Yes, I have. We have planned to visit him sometime this year. Max said you guys had been married for seventeen years." Sarah smiled. "That's awesome."

"That's true, but separated for the past eight years. He has proceeded to fulfil his life in California with his girlfriend of ten years."

Sarah thought to herself. *I would have never known they were separated because Max speaks so highly of them.*

"May I ask what happen? I heard you say he was with his girlfriend of ten years."

"Honestly, I rather not say."

"That's fine. I understand."

"I can tell you truly love Max. Max loves you too. I've never heard him talk about a woman like he talks about you. I am happy for you both. You mentioned that Max said he would retire in a couple of years. I hate to tell you this, but that's a lie. That's what he has done most of his life. He may give it up for a month or two, and then he will go back to it. I'm not trying to discourage you, but you may want to think about what you're getting yourself into before you marry Max."

Sarah looked up at Amy, "what do you mean?"

"I put my dreams on hold to raise our children. I never had to worry about money. Corey always made sure the kids and I were taken care of, but he was never home. I use to travel with him before we had kids. I had to stop when the kids became old enough to attend school. I couldn't keep taking them out of school every time Corey received a call to go out of town to work. I could see our relationship fading over time. Corey developed bad drug and drinking habits; no matter what I did, I couldn't make him stay with me. He eventually got another woman. She called me introduced herself as his woman and said that he wanted her to tell me to stop looking and waiting for him to come back home because his home was no longer with me but with her. I didn't say anything. I already knew it was over before it was actually over; I was waiting for closure. We stop talking to each other completely. When the kids became teenagers, they went to stay with their dad. We probably will never get a divorce, which is fine with me. If anything would ever happen to him, everything he has would go to the kids and me. I'm content; I can go after my dreams now. All I'm saying sweetheart, being married to an Ironworker is not going to be easy. You have to be willing to forgive quickly. Love each other more than you did the day before, step outside of your comfort zone. Do something different and unexpected; create memories as a couple and a family. Keep the fire burning so that no one on the outside can send a strong wind and blow it out. You never know when he may get laid off and have to go out of town to work. Be prepared to be a single mom with excellent benefits because he's not going to be able to raise your girls the way he could have if he were always at home. Be prepared to explain to your children why their daddy wasn't there for their birthday party. Has he missed any birthdays yet?" asked Amy.

"Yes, once or twice," Sarah replied softly. She was trying to push back the overwhelming emotions that arose because of what Amy shared with her.

"I truly appreciate what you have told me. And I know as long as we keep God first, we will be able to withstand any storm that comes our way. I know when I marry him, I will be marrying into the industry he loves so much, and I don't mind that as long as the girls and I are his main priority. I would never stop him for wanting to provide for us even if this means I have to wait a while before I can see him." Sarah said with confidence as she looked at Amy.

But Sarah would soon regret everything she said to Amy regarding Max's industry.

"This is true; I will make sure I keep you all lifted in prayer," Amy said disappointed.

Sarah knew she would have to pray harder about her and Max's relationship. She could just imagine what Amy's prayers about them would be.

When Max got home from work, he showed Sarah New York City Ironworkers pay scale. The Ironworker book indicated that he would be making $42.50 an hour, with $2.00 going toward his pension, and $20.00 goes into his vacation fund (this was per day).

Max left for New York three days after receiving a call about the job there. He had to work in New York for at least two months before he could come home to visit. Sarah wanted to visit Max after two weeks of him being in New York, so she did. She did a little site seeing and spent some time with Max when he got off of work. She stayed three days, then caught the early flight back home. She made it home just in time to make it to church. Sarah sat through service with all smiles. After service was over, Sarah walked up to Bishop Edwards and First Lady Edwards to greet them.

"Hey Bishop." Sarah smiled.

"Well hello daughter. Nice to see you made it home safe." Bishop Edwards gave Sarah a hug.

Sarah walked over to First Lady Edwards and gave her a hug.

"Sarah come here." Yelled Bishop Edwards. He crossed his arms than stroked his chin. "You better stop and keep it holy."

Sarah mouth dropped. "Huh? What Bishop? What did I do?"

"You know God reveals things to me concerning his children."

"Ok." Sarah walked away. She didn't have to think hard about what he was talking about. She didn't think she and Max would get in trouble for clothes burning.

Since Sarah no longer worked at the salon, she decided to start a mobile nail tech company. She went to her clients' houses to cater to their hands and feet. When Sarah's faithful client who attended the church and the prayer line found out she no longer worked at the shop, he signed up for her mobile nail tech service. He was getting a manicure and pedicure every two weeks; then he started getting them done every week. He was tipping her five times the amount of the cost she charged for nail care services. It took Sarah a while to figure out what was happening. She always tried to give people the benefit of the doubt. The more she saw her client, the more uncomfortable she became. Everyone knew that Sarah's client had the hots for her except for her. She talked to First Lady Edwards about what was going on. She told her she had to let him know that his behavior was inappropriate. Sarah did just that, but that didn't stop him from coming to church to prey on her. When she saw him, she would run and hide or leave early to avoid seeing him. He would get on the prayer line and pray for Sarah and a wife. Sarah sat on the line in silence. She didn't want him to hear her breathe. She had a strong feeling that he was hoping that Sarah would be his wife. Sarah didn't tell Max about what was going on because she wasn't sure what he was going to do. So she did the only thing she knew to do and prayed about it. On Sunday morning, Sarah got up to get her and the kids dress for church. On their way out the door Haven threw up everywhere. She had a temperature of 102. Sarah didn't go to church. She changed clothes and took Haven to the doctor. The doctor informed her she had a stomach virus and that it would pass in a couple of days. When Sarah got home she received a call from Bishop Edwards.

"Hey, Bishop."

"Hey daughter, were you at church today?"

"No, I had to take Haven to the doctor. She has a stomach virus."

"Okay. I saw your client today. I told him that he could not come in my church with that lustful spirit, preying on my daughter. I said man she not stunting you. She about to get married. That's what I was calling to tell you. You won't have to worry about him anymore. He wasn't coming to seek God; he was seeking you."

"Thank you Bishop. Love you."

"Love you too, daughter. I'll talk to you later."

Sarah didn't see or hear from her client again.

For Sarah, waiting on Max to come home to visit was intense, especially with her having wedding fever. Now that she and Max were both saved, filled with the Holy Spirit, and living for God, she felt it was only right to tie the knot immediately. At this point, things were really looking great for Sarah and Max. Sarah was enthusiastic about how everything had come together. However, that joy didn't last for long. Sarah posted on Facebook saying, "It's crazy how before we got saved we would sing songs like, 'He's mine you may have had him once but I got him all the time.' What kind of foolishness is this? "After that post, Sarah received a message in her inbox.

"Lol, I bet you feel real stupid right now. You stole Max from me now he cheating on you. Stupid Trick." Stated the message.

"I'd rather not go there with you. Max and I are happy. I was referring to a song. Have a good day. God Bless."

"You on Facebook acting like you so saved. Trick you ain't saved because if you were, you wouldn't have been talking to Max and you knew he had a girlfriend."

Sarah didn't know Max had a girlfriend. At the time, she didn't care because they weren't dating; they were just getting to know each other as friends. It wasn't until Max's ex-girlfriend called Sarah to see who she was after finding Sarah's number along with text messages in his phone. Sarah explained to her that they weren't dating. Sarah would never have taken Max serious. His ex-girlfriend did the unthinkable: she told Sarah that she asked Max if he would have meet Sarah first before meeting her, would he have chosen Sarah over her and Max said he would have without thinking twice.

"I just want to take this time to apologize to you for anything I have done to hurt you." Sarah typed.

"Trick, I don't want no apology."

"The person you are looking for is no longer a part of me. I can't change the past. Like I stated once before, Max and I are happy. Stop in boxing me please."

Sarah couldn't understand why his ex was still holding a grudge towards her. She just got married. How can she possibly still be thinking about Max? Sarah could have stopped this circus act way before it started if she had in boxed Max's ex-girlfriend husband and let him know what she was doing, but she didn't, so the show went on.

"Tell Max I said what's up-- me and his baby girl are doing fine."

Sarah heart melted. She couldn't believe what she had just read.

"You all don't have a baby together. He told me you lost your baby."

"He lied to you. Go on my page and look through my pictures. My baby looks just like him. Take your time. I'll wait."

Sarah went to her page and looked through her pictures. While looking through her pictures, Sarah became confused. She wanted to cry fire. She became so mad with Max. The baby looked just like their daughter, Haven.

"How does he know this baby is his?"

"Trust, he knows. He has enough to know."

"We want a blood test. We'll pay for it."

"No, I don't want a blood test! For what? This his baby!"

"How can he be there for his child if he doesn't know it's his? I want to know because we are about to get married and I don't want any loss ends that could be tied now."

"Don't worry about us because we don't want anything to do with him. We won't put child support on him or you, lol."

"So why would you tell me you have a baby by him if you don't want anything to do with him?"

"Because it's not about him; it's about you. I want you to know that as long as I have his baby, I will always be a part of his life."

Sarah did something she promised herself she would never

do. She called Max while he was at work. She knew how dangerous his job was, and if he accumulated just a little stress, he could endanger himself and others due to his lack of focus. When Max answered the phone, she told him everything his ex- girlfriend said. Max denied everything. He kept calm and told her he will talk to her when he got off work. Sarah really didn't have much to talk to Max about because she knew it was a possibility that could be his baby. She recalled the night she stayed up waiting on him to come home. He told her he was at the hospital with his ex and that she had lost their baby. Sarah didn't communicate with Max for several days. Max decided to do his own investigation by calling around, but he didn't know Sarah went search for clues also. Sarah questioned God about the situation. She asked God, "Why is all of this happening. Why now? He reminded her of a sermon someone preached at her church. The pastor said, "There are things in your life waiting to be resolved, but it's not time yet. When it's time for you to deal with it, God will show you how."

Lauren's aunt Martha called to talk to talk to Sarah because she had seen that Sarah was at church physically but her mind was far from it.

"Hello?" Sarah turned over on her back as she laid on the couch.

"Hey Sarah! This is Martha. How are you doing?"

"I'm doing ok, and you?"

"I'm great. I wanted to talk to you at church, but you left before I made it over to you. I have been thinking about you nonstop. You know what they say when you think about someone like that: you need to pray for them or reach out to them. So what's been going on?"

Sarah told Martha what happen with Max's ex-girlfriend. She explained to her that she doesn't think she should marry Max and that God may be telling her not to marry him.

"Look don't trip off of her she is probably lying. What woman don't want the child's father to be in their life? That's stupid. She sounds like she's crazy."

"She is very crazy. She used to call my phone and leave me text messages on my phone. She stalked me when I stayed with my mom. She stalked us when we moved here; she looked up my name, found out where I stayed, and left a note on my car for Max. She called a dateline number acting like me; she listed my number and had men calling me."

"Huh, yeah that girl nutty as a fruit cake. She's a non-factor. As for as knowing if Max is the man God want you to marry-- you need to fast and pray about that because you don't want to get married then file for divorce. God doesn't like divorce. I've been divorced before, and I will tell you this: I wouldn't wish that on my worst enemy. A divorce is like a death that you keep reliving. It kills you mentally, spiritually, emotionally; physically, you're torn and divided like your things has to be during court. It took me a while to recover. There is life after divorce, but it's best to avoid it. I'll be praying for you Sarah. I love you."

"Thank you. I love you too."

After getting off the phone with Martha, Sarah fast and prayed for a several weeks. She went back to investigating Max's ex-girlfriend's allegations. She searched through Max's ex's pictures and friends' profiles on Facebook for several days, looking for clues about the baby. She was successful. Sarah found out that the baby Max's ex-girlfriend claimed to be Max's wasn't even her baby but her grandbaby. Sarah's anger caused her to believe the baby looked like Haven. Max called Sarah and informed her that he talked to his ex-girlfriend's brother, and he told him that she was never pregnant. The baby was her granddaughter. But that then raised a question about Max being at the hospital with her during her alleged miscarriage. He admitted he lied. He said he wasn't at the hospital at all but at the casino gambling. Both Sarah and Max were relieved.

Max drove home from New York once he reached his two-month requirement. Sarah couldn't believe it. Her Lil Daddy was finally home. She felt as though they haven't seen each other in years, not to mention being up close and virtual. They couldn't contain themselves-- rather they didn't want to. They willingly gave into their flesh the day before their wedding.

Feeling relaxed and excited Sarah, and Max arrived at their church Saturday afternoon. They met their Bishop in his office before gathering in the sanctuary for their big day. Bishop Edwards did a quick recap of their marriage counseling session they had with him and First Lady Edwards's months ago, insuring they didn't have second thoughts about getting married.

"Hey daughter, so are you ready to get married?" Bishop Edwards asked. He formed a big playful smile.

Sarah smiled. "Yes, I am." She looked over at Max feeling grateful.

Bishop Edwards hugged Sarah. He stepped back slightly and held her by both of her arms. He looked at her with curiosity. "Are you pregnant?"

"No. I'm just fat." Sarah laughed loudly. "Why did you say that?" Sarah took a minute to ponder on what he asked. She knew he was a Godly man and that God reveals things to him.

"How do you know you're not pregnant?"

Sarah looked over at First Lady Edwards.

First Lady Edwards sat on the edge of her seat awaiting Sarah's response. She was hoping Sarah took her advice on keeping the goodies in the bag until after the wedding.

Sarah smiled; her body tingled as she had a flashback of yesterday. Her response was uncertain. "I'm not."

"Are you ready, young man?" Bishop Edwards approached Max and shook his hand.

"Yes, sir. I told myself if I ever got Sarah, I would put a crown on her head and treat her as my queen," said Max.

"I heard that young man. You better handle my daughter right, and that means a lot of TLC." Bishop Edwards gave Max a mean expression, accompanied by a pleasant grin.

Max, Bishop and First Lady Edwards, and Sarah headed to the sanctuary. Bishop Edwards stood in front of Sarah and

Max in the pulpit; Max and Sarah stood facing Bishop with their backs facing a host of Sarah's family and friends who came to support them. They glanced at each other, smiling.

"Dearly beloved, we are gathered here today to join this man, Max Houston, and this woman, Sarah Strive in holy matrimony."

"Yes!" Sarah shouted, nervous.

"Not yet." chuckled Bishop Edwards.

"Oh, I'm sorry."

"Do you take this man to be your husband?"

"I do." Sarah just smiled.

"To live together in matrimony. To love, honor, and cherish."

"I do."

"Not just yet, daughter. She is ready, brother. She has waited long enough." Bishop Edwards said to Sarah's dad, who sitting along the front row.

Sarah smiled with embarrassment as the sanctuary filled with laughter. Two things were obvious: she hasn't been to many weddings, and she was nervous as heck.

Bishop Edwards continued, "Comfort him and keep him in sickness and health and forsaking all others for as long as you both shall live? Daughter, this is it."

"I do," Sarah smiled at Max and blinked back her tears, refusing to destroy her makeup before she took pictures.

Bishop Edwards turned to Max. He smiled and said. "Are you ready to read your wedding vows, son?"

"Yes, sir." Max cleared his throat; he was feeling content and positive.

"Dreams are made to come true with much-needed prayer and faith to push them through. I know that now because you're here, and I can't stop staring at you. You stepped out of my dreams and into my life. That's why I'm exceedingly proud to call you my wife. I never thought this day would come even after I had realized you were the one. You help shape me into the Godly man I am today, forcing me to put aside my childish ways. I knew you deserved better; that's why I had no problem with writing you this letter. When I look at you, I see hope, happiness, peace, success, love and kindness all of which you restored in me. I made a vow to God that if he allows me to marry you, I'll never cheat, lie, mistreat or neglect you for as long as we both shall live."

Sarah released what seemed like a backed up-stream of tears on her purple dress. Max stood with gladness in his eyes.

In an effort to silence their bawling, their guests reached for the tissues.

"Good job, son." Bishop Edwards cleared his throat and continued with the ceremony.

"Repeat after me. I, Max Houston, take you, Sarah Strive, to be my wife. To have and to hold from this day forward, for better, for worse, for richer, for poorer, in sickness and in health to love and to cherish 'til death do us part."

"Sarah repeat after me" said, Bishop Edwards. I, Sarah Strive, take you, Max Houston, to be my husband. To have and to hold from this day forward, for better, for worse, for richer, for poorer in sickness and in health to love and to cherish 'til death do us part."

"Max, place the ring onto her finger and repeat after me," instructed Bishop Edwards. "I give you this ring as a token and pledge of our constant faith and abiding love." Max winked at Sarah.

"Sarah, place the ring onto Max's finger and repeat after me," instructed Bishop Edwards. "I give you this ring as a token and pledge of our constant faith and abiding love." Sarah winked several times at Max, smiling.

"I now ask that you both hold hands. We have come together in this place and have heard the willingness Max and Sarah to be joined in marriage. They have come of their own free will and in our hearing have made a covenant of faithfulness. They have given and received rings as the seal of their promises. Is there anyone that feel these two should not be married, speak now or forever hold your peace."

"Hold up," a loud voice sounded from outside the door.

The middle aisle entry doors swung open.

Everyone was floored with confusion, even the groom. People began to whisper. "Who the heck is that guy? I've never seen him before today." The man cried out, "Please Sarah don't ruin your life because of me. I still love you. I'm sorry things didn't work out between us as you would have liked them to, but, I can't stand to see you with him." Max blinked his eyes only to find that he was woolgathering.

"Since there be none, by virtue of the authority vested in me under the law of the state of Missouri, I now pronounce you--

"Wait!" a spineless, yet loud voice shouted from the back of the church. A woman with a big yellow sunflower hat stood up. She took off her hat to reveal herself. "Sarah, I hate you! You stole Max from me. I would love to interrupt this appalling wedding and save you the future embarrassment. You should not marry Max. We are still sleeping together. Oh, by the way, I'm carrying his baby. Did you enjoy last night Maxi boy?" The woman licked her lips seductively. "Just know that he will never leave me alone, married or not because you can never replace me. You can never be me. Huh, replacing me will never be easy. For him. Mrs. Sarah wants to be, but will never live up to be Houston. Stupid trick."

"Sarah, you can kiss your groom, now," said Bishop Edwards interrupting her wild daydream.

Max and Sarah kissed.

"What kind of kiss is that, you're married now? You guys have to do better than that. I need to see some tongue, saliva, whichever one comes first." Bishop Edwards laughed, awaiting the grand finale. Sarah realized seeing Max's stalker, psycho, ex-girlfriend was just her imagination trying to get the best of her. Max and Sarah kissed as if it would be their final one. Sarah's lips had become sacred, sealed with a stamp that said property of Max Houston. Do not tamper or you will be dealt with accordingly. When Max kissed Sarah, she was officially sold. She was withdrawn from the market never to be handled by another human again, and so was Max. Their constant reminder along with others were their rings; they are to be worn at all times. The receipt was their marriage license. They were like antique glass-- fragile, irreplaceable. Sarah was a tangible item that would only operate correctly if Max utilized the right instructions. Max was an action figure, hard on the outside, but easy to damage if Sarah didn't handle with caution. Both of their instruction manual came from the Bible.

They took several pictures with friends and family after the wedding. Max stopped to admire Sarah as his wife while she posed in her smoking hot wedding dress. It was a slimming purple dress with gold sparkles. A gold band accompanied the strap. It had a split that started at her thigh and stopped below her ankle. She wore a pair of six inch sparkling gold heels. Her hair color was auburn with a hint of white blond and gold blond. Her hair was curled and pinned to the side opposite of her strap. Her makeup was flawless, as if she didn't have any on. Max blew Sarah a kiss. She smiled then sized him up also. Max's hair was nicely faded. His facial hairs were trimmed to perfection. He had on grey slacks with a purple collared button up shirt accompanied by a grey blazer with a purple handkerchief in his top pocket.

Oh, how I love that man, Sarah thought to herself.

There was no fancy reception after the wedding. Sarah, Max, Hannah, and Haven went to Crackle Barrel restaurant to grab a bite to eat before going home. They needed all the sleep they could obtain. New York was a fifteen-hour drive from Saint Louis. That was a total of 1,600 miles in motion before they arrived at their honeymoon destination not including the stops they may make in between.

CHAPTER SEVEN

Their alarm clock sounded promptly at five o'clock a.m. only to be silenced for another thirty minutes. Max always took advantage of the additional thirty minutes of sleep; he proclaimed it's the best investment he could ever make for himself. Sarah and Max dropped Hannah and Haven off at Sarah mom's house at seven thirty a.m. They headed toward the highway merging onto interstate seventy eastbound. Their honeymoon had officially started.

They have driven out of town together on several occasions with the longest trip being an eight-hour drive but nothing more. They came prepared with fruit, pre-made turkey and ham sandwiches, chips, and the only candy bar they both could agree on: Snickers. They had an array of music to choose from. Max refused to let Sarah drive, exposing his trait of always wanting to be in control. To Sarah, the first seven hours of riding seemed like infinity. Their fifteen- hour romantic newlywed road trip turned into a nonstop emotional roller coaster ride filled with plenty of surprises that kept their ears on offense mode. Their reactions were far from being quick to listen, slow to speak and slow to anger. They became instant fools, as they allowed one another to provoke their spirits to anger. They argued for one hour if not more. They spent two and a half hours not speaking to each other, leaving room for the enemy to come in and tie up the strong man so that he may destroy their house. It wasn't a shock to Sarah when they realized they had been driving the wrong way for two hours due to Max being stubborn and not wanting to ask Sarah for help. She couldn't allow the madness between them to go on, so she apologized to Max, even though she felt like he caused most of their arguments with his nonchalant attitude. They used Sarah's professional background along with Max GPS system to make it to New York.

Their eyes lit up when they saw the New York welcome sign. Sarah was amazed; she had never seen something beautiful at night. She looked for a woman who resides on the island of her own surrounded by beautiful water. The prettiest woman she had ever laid eyes on other than herself--the Statute of Liberty. Sarah turned and looked at Max, giving him a big smile of excitement. Max grabbed her hand and pulled her toward him and kissed her. While riding through the streets of New York, Max saw fit to put on Alicia Keys song "New York", featuring Jay-Z. They both began to sing and dance as it became hard to resist.

"Oh, New York, Oh New York. If I could make it here. I could make it anywhere that's what they say. I got a pocket full of dreams, baby we in New York. These streets will make you feel brand new big lights will inspire you." Sarah meditated on those words as she sang the song over and again.

"We in New York baby," Max said shouting out the car window as he drove 85 miles per hour down the slightly empty highway.

That moment Sarah felt as if she had accomplished everything she wanted to achieve in her life, even if her track sheet showed she had achieved nothing. They wouldn't have never thought they would be in New York City out of all places. There was no doubt in their mind that God made all this possible for them.

They couldn't stay at Max's place in New York because two of his friends shared an apartment with him on the other side of town in Brooklyn. Once they arrived in New York, they drove a little further to New Jersey. There they stayed at the Rivera hotel. The hotel came highly recommended by a friend of Max's who recently visited there. Sarah wasn't to pleased about the hotel, but she knew if she wanted to shop the Rivera would have to do for now. The commute from the hotel to Max's job at the Twin Towers wasn't that far away. The hotels in New Jersey were much cheaper than New York. Max had one more day to spend with Sarah before he went back to work. Then she would be left alone to explore the beautiful streets of New York and New Jersey. After checking into their hotel room, they blended with the bed for guiltless rest.

The next morning, they woke up smiling at one another. They embraced the peace of mind that kept them from feeling weighed down because of the sin called fornication that habitually held them in bondage. Max wanted to surprise Sarah by stepping outside their usual routine which was take out and a movie from Red Box. A close friend of Max's told him about a company named "Intimate Expression" located in New York City. The company specializes in wedding planning along with romantic plan for date nights. They wasted no time getting dressed, considering the time zone change. They left the hotel after having breakfast that consisted of scrambled eggs with cheese, pancakes, bacon, hash browns and orange juice. Sarah wore a peach and gray loose fitted dress that had one long sleeve. She placed a gray belt around her waist to give the dress some appeal. The dress stopped slightly above her knee. She accessorized with silver and completed her outfit with grey shoes that matched her belt. Her clutch was grey and peach. It matched her dress perfectly. She thought she looked good if she had to say so herself. Max wore black button up collar shirt with a light grey blazer and a black handkerchief that stuck out of his blazer top pocket. He wore dark blue jeans accompanied by one of his favorite NBA player's shoes, Jordan six rings, they were black, venom green, white, and cement grey. This look on Max did something to Sarah; she loved to see him in tennis shoes and a blazer, simple look, but it has playboy written all over it.

Their first destination was screaming high above New York City, on the Roosevelt Island Tram. It was a five minute air ride that seemed like a twenty minute roller coaster ride that has not dropped down the intense slope. Sarah held onto Max the entire time, looking over the tall bridges, water and cars that appeared smaller. She was terrified. Max, however, loved it. His work as an Ironworker requires him to be one hundred feet in the air and sometimes underground, he has helped build array of buildings and bridges.

Ironworkers are the bravest of the brave. Max along with other men and women risk their life daily so that people can have a place to work and live. Sarah thought it was cute hearing Max talk about how beautiful the bridges were. When Sarah tells people what he does for a living they always ask if she fears for his life. Her responds remain the same: "No, we both are strong believers in Christ. We always pray. We know that God has him covered." She informed them that because so many people have lost their lives because of massive heart attacks, strokes, overheating, metal beams falling on them and other things. Max stayed on top of his skills in his profession. Also, he's an inch away from being admitted for being a health nut. Sarah admitted that she would need to put herself into a psych ward if she always worried about Max's wellbeing at work.

The ride on the Roosevelt Tram ended near the New York Double Decker Bus which was their next destination. The light breeze brushed their faces as they rode on the roof of the bus.

They observed the assortment of people that lived in New York City. They found New York to be very busy. They agreed it wasn't a place they could ever grow fond of; Sarah couldn't imagine toting Hannah and Haven around in the big city, catching buses and trains. Even though the streets are not constantly filled with cabs as people watch in the movies. It's never anywhere to park, or parking is extremely expensive, $25 an hour and upwards--try paying that every day. The jobs pay well. The clothes come cheap, but the price of a soda is unbelievable. The cost of one bedroom apartment in New York is the cost of a five bedroom house in the suburban area of Saint Louis. Although, with any states certain parts are cheaper than others, like New Jersey is inexpensive to live in versus New York.

They walked the streets of Times Square, shopping and people watching. They went to the movies in Times Square. It was a pleasant experience, New York experience. The cinema was huge. It had escalators that led up to the concession stand and movie room. The seats were comfy, and the screen was

3D. If you reached your hand out, it appeared as if you could touch the screen. The surround sound enhanced the overall film experience. They rode the subway from Times Square to their final destination. While on the exceedingly crowded subway where they were lucky to get a seat, they missed their stop to Bateaux, New York. They didn't realize they had missed their stop even with Max and Sarah being the only two on the subway. The subway came to a complete stop. The conductor had walked throughout the subway before he noticed Sarah and Max were still on the train.

"Ah!" the conductor screamed when he saw them. "What are you two still doing on the train? You have reached the end." The conductor said looking weird.

Max and Sarah smiled at each other. "We were waiting to get off at Bateaux, New York," Sarah said giggling. She observed the motionless trains surrounding them.

"Well, you missed it. That was the last stop. I'm going to take a quick break before I go back that way. You all can wait on the train." said the conductor.

"Ok, thanks." replied Max.

As if they had a choice, the train pulled into a subway station surrounded by other trains. The only way out was the way they came.

"I bet that the man is talking about us. Who in the world gets stuck on the train?" Sarah laughed. She smiled at Max and grabbed his hand.

"It was your fault," said Max.

"Really! Max," Sarah looked in shock. "You should know where you're going! You ride this train every day."

Max smiled. Sarah smiled back. She stood up in front of Max facing him. She zoned out allowing her mind to take a bizarre trip.

"Oh, Daddy, you know what would be nice right about now?" Sarah smiled.

"What's that baby doll?" Max tried to keep his body under subjection.

"If you…" Sarah whispered into Max's ear.

He smiled as his eyes and heart became stationary.

"So, how about it? I just need a minute." Sarah became eager just to take what she wanted.

"What? no! We on a subway in New York. I could lose my job. Wait till we get back to the hotel." Max kissed Sarah on her forehead. "Ok?."

Sarah sat in silence with disappointment on the rise. The train jerked and proceeded to move.

He has to come off that because Biblically his body is mine. He no longer has authority over it, Sarah thought to herself.

They exited the train at the first train stop. She distinguished her feelings so they could enjoy the rest of their night together in peace with limited distraction. They arrived promptly at the unique restaurant. The server seated them. The boat sailed as they waited on their food. It was a new experience for the both of them. They could see the Statue of Liberty along with beautiful buildings and bridges. They thought the food was fantastic. A day to remember. They ended their day back at the hotel. They were exhausted. Sarah fell to sleep in Max's arms. Max took Sarah clothes off and placed her underneath the covers.

The next morning, Sarah was awakened by a text.

Good morning, Baby Doll.

I didn't want to wake you when I left for work. I just wanted to let you know that I love you with all my heart. I truly enjoyed you yesterday. I was looking forward to last night, but you fell asleep. Be ready for me when I get off work. Oh, and I left you thirteen hundred dollars inside the nightstand drawer. Have fun shopping.

Sarah shopped until her feet was begging for a heated massage in Epson salt. She arrived back at the hotel just in time to freshen up before Max came. Throughout the room, Sarah lit scented candles that filled the room with an aroma of comfort.

While preparing her mind mentally in hopes that her body

would follow, Sarah closed her eyes and pictured Max. Her starvation from yesterday had her envisioning Max was already there. Her thoughts and emotions went on a rampage. Sarah was clearly unaware of Max's presence.

"Dang," said Max. He stood in shock. "After being exposed to Sarah's sinful pleasure. I would be lying if I said it didn't make me feel some type of way about what you were doing; you couldn't wait until I made it here?"

"Oh, baby I'm sorry. If it makes you feel any better, I was thinking about you." Sarah smiled.

"Man, how do I know that?" Max twisted his mouth in sarcastic disbelief.

"Oh, baby, you have me on the edge and sadly I've connected myself to the cables getting ready to jump."

"I can't say that I think you're telling the truth. Now how would you feel if you caught me? "

"Ugh I don't know, probably mad and disgusted," Sarah said feeling weird.

"My point exactly." Max shook his head.

"That was just an appetizer. I'm ready for the main course." Sarah grabbed Max by the hand and walked into the bedroom.

"Wait!" shouted Max. "Are you going to do this now? I can't get over what I just saw. You just set a sensual standard that I wouldn't dare compete with."

"Awe baby, well maybe you will knock next time." Sarah smiled. "No, but in all honesty, you will never be able to satisfy me like I can satisfy myself. Unless of course I sit and tell you all my fantasies."

"You know, I would never think about it like that. If you walk me through it, telling me where your triggers are your likes and dislikes, and I promise I will make all your fantasies come true." Max gently rubbed the back of Sarah's neck.

"Likewise, I want to make all your fantasies come true as long as they don't involve a third person. Keep in mind, I'm strictly Max." Sarah said displaying a serious face. "I will never understand why men want to have a threesome when they can barely keep up with one woman. Not to mention it's a horrible sin."

"The only woman I want is you." Max reassured Sarah.

I wonder if masturbation is a sin also, given that you're envisioning your spouse. I guess that's something I'll have to research, Sarah pondered to herself.

"Deal, however, it doesn't take much to please me." Max laughed.

"Hmm, that's what you think. I'm that play you didn't see coming. There are things I can and will do to you to make you hooked. You would need to check into a rehabilitation center."

"Well, enough talk," Max put his index finger on Sarah's lips. "Let me make one of your many fantasies come true. I married the woman of my dreams, and we have our whole lives to bring our fantasies into reality."

They utilized the entire night doing just that.

Sadly, after a jaw-dropping experience, Sarah and Max's two-week honeymoon had come to an end. She stuffed her luggage with jewelry, clothes, and shoes that she purchased from New York. She flew back home to tend to their children and her job that seems to malfunction when she's away. Sarah's plane landed safely in Saint Louis. When her feet touch the pavement, her vacation pass had expired, and her daily duties reactivated.

Sarah knew the importance of keeping her marriage off life support, especially in the first stage. She made frequent trips to New York to spend time with Max; it was easiest for her to visit him than him visiting them due to Max seven day, ten-hour work schedule. Unfortunately, Sarah didn't bring the girls along with her because they were attending school at the time. Sarah enjoyed herself and Max every time she visited New York. There was always something to see and do. One day, Sarah arranged a last minute trip to see Max for the weekend. She was missing him. She dropped Hannah and Haven off at her mother's house, and Evans dropped her off at the airport. Sarah didn't have any luggage to check in, so she boarded the plane promptly. She brought along three undergarment sets that arranged neatly in her purse. Once Sarah arrived at Newark Airport, her taxi driver was waiting on her.

Sarah and Max established a feasible relationship with the taxi driver. They called him personally whenever Sarah was in town. Due to Max's work schedule and the massive New Jersey traffic, it was impossible for Max to pick her up from the airport or drop her off. The cab driver dropped her off in front of the Rivera hotel. They always stayed in when she visits. Max paid for the room before her arrival, so Sarah checked in and headed to their room. She sang and danced down the long hallway. She placed her purse and room key on the dresser after entering the room. She walked over to the bed and fell onto it; she closed her eyes and just laid there.

After lying down for a while, a warm kiss compressed her lips. Her body went into attack mode. Her heart pounded as sweat raced to the surface of her skin.

"Did I scare you? I'm sorry. I didn't mean to."

"What are you doing here?" asked Sarah feeling more frighten than pleased.

"You're not happy to see me are you?"

"Of course I am why else would I fly across the world to see you?"

"Aw, baby I miss you too. I didn't mean to scare you. Promise." Max said gently. He gave Sarah a long hug.

"I thought you were at work."

"I was. I'm an hour ahead of you remember. But I did take off tomorrow so I can spend time with you. We can check out that the church you wanted to visit."

Often times Sarah didn't make it to church whenever she came to visit Max in New York. She hated missing church, but she was married now. She knew this was a sacrifice she had to make. She was pleased to know they were going to attend church tomorrow. They left out early Saturday morning. They drove Max's car instead of riding the bus or catching the subway. They planned to attend church that Saturday night.

They shopped all day practically. Max has never been an extended hour shopper, so after three hours of shopping, he was ready to go back to the room to get dressed for church. However, there was another store Sarah had to visit. She saw the prettiest shoes for Hannah. She did not want to leave without them because she knew she was not going to find those same shoes in Saint Louis, so she asked Max to stop by the store, but he refused. Sarah put her head down slightly and started to pout. Max glanced at Sarah from out the corner of his eye. He hated to see her upset, especially knowing he was the cause of it. He gave into her silent temper tantrum.

Boom! The car came to a complete stop after Max, slammed on the breaks in the middle of the street. Sarah's eyes grew large with confusion. The tires screeched as he proceeded to make a u-turn along one of the busiest streets in New Jersey, Broadway. Max looked over at Sarah and smiled as his juvenile behavior conveyed involuntary attention to them. Max made a left at the first traffic light. They heard people screaming and honking their horns at them. They were puzzled as to why people were reacting this way, but before they could figure out the reason, they heard sirens. They looked around and saw police lights flashing behind them telling them to pull over. Max immediately pulled over along the shopping strip. The police officer walked up to the car asking for driver license, insurance, and vehicle registration. Max frantically looked into the arm rest for the information the police requested. It didn't take a rocket scientist to figure out Max didn't get pulled over often. He couldn't find it, so he asked Sarah to look inside the glove box for proof of insurance and registration. Sarah pulled out the vehicle's insurance and registration form to the car. She passed them to Max. Max then handed the essential information the police officer. The officer looked aggressively into the car. Sarah sat in silence, observing his partner walk around the car, while taking mental notes.

Sarah heard the officer say, "The reason I pulled you over was because you turned on the street that prohibits turning of any kind. That is why all those people were honking their horns at you. We watched you the entire time as we sat at the corner. Give me a minute to run your information through the system. Sit tight, I'll be back." The officer then walked back to his car.

As they sat in the car, a man in a red beat-up pickup truck pulled beside Max and Sarah. He stuck his head out the window. "I was trying to tell you that you couldn't turn there," the man shouted. He shook his head in an irritated fashion before driving away.

Sarah prayed as they waited. She observed Max as he shook his head in disbelief.

The police officer came back to the car and said, "I'm going to have to ask you both to get out of the vehicle." In shock, they both got out of the car.

"Oh, Lord, I cannot go to prison in New York," Sarah mumbled. She glanced over the crowd that stood nearby protesting that the police officer leave them the Heck alone.

Max was thinking he would get fired, had he got thrown in jail. His police record was spotless. One reason was that of his job. One scratch (ticket) could prevent him from getting his next job. The other reason was that he was a part of a concealed association that looked out for each other.

The police officer went on to say. "I ran your name, along with the car into the system. Even though you have accurate insurance, you failed to register your car within the required thirty days of purchase. You do not have the proper license plates on this car."

"Excuse me, Officer Mack, the license plates belong to him. They belong to another vehicle." Sarah said politely.

The officer disfigured his face, "So he took the plates off another car he owns to put on this car."

"Yes," Sarah shook her head with desperation.

The officer sighed, "That's illegal in the state of New York and probably in the forty-nine other states too. I could take him to jail."

Sarah could tell Max wanted just to faint.

"Lucky for you, I will just tow your car, I will refrain from sending you to jail. I encourage you to remove your belongings from the car. A tow truck is on its way."

They did as the officer requested.

"Here is the information to the towing company. They will give instructions on how to get your car out the pound. Your court date is next month; failure to appear will cause a warrant issued out for your arrest."

Max took the papers.

Sarah thanked the officer for not locking them up.

The car was towed from the premises in front of the crowd. Max hid his embarrassment by holding his head down. It was obvious that he wanted to do a disappearing act and vanish to some place other than here, whereas Sarah did not care; she knew they did not know her, and would probably never see them again, yet her heart was torn because of Max. She knew how much he loved that car, even though he only drove it to get groceries and do his laundry while he was in New York. Sarah could not help but think this was her fault. As they walked, Sarah felt as though she was walking the plank to her doom. They walked three long city blocks before getting on the bus only to get off five minutes later because they were closer to the hotel than they thought. Sarah assumed the bus driver thought they were playing on the bus because she passed their stop after they rang the bell twice to get off the bus. Fortunately, she let them off at the next stop which wasn't too far from the hotel.

Once they arrived at the hotel, they took the first elevator going up to the thirteenth floor. From there, they crossed ten rooms before they made it to their room. Max opened the hotel room door and allowed Sarah to go in first. Max laid across the bed disturbed and stiff as he allowed the bags to fall off his fingers onto the hotel floor. Despite being exhausted from their crazy day, Sarah was still anticipating going to church. She sat her bags on the table before going into the bathroom to take a quick shower. She noticed Max still lying on the bed when she came out of the bathroom. He looked severely wounded. Sarah instantly knew he did not want to attend church anymore, even though she felt they needed to go especially after what happen, yet she refused to say anything to Max. She made a conscious decision to stay with him in the hotel instead of going to church, even though she was looking forward to going all day.

Max couldn't overlook the detailed disappointment written on Sarah's face.

"Bay, now why in the world did you tell the police officer that the plates did not go to that car. You said, 'excuse me, those license plates are registered to his other car.' I dropped my head and said, 'oh Lord, they gon' take us to jail for sure'." Max smiled. "I love my wife."

They both laughed relieving some of the stress they had acquired.

"Hey, I thought that would help so it didn't seem as we stole the plates nor the car." Sarah smiled feeling a little embarrassed. Thanks to Max, she acknowledged her commitment to being honest almost got them put under the jail with no bail.

Sarah explored her shopping bags in hopes to fit all the clothes she bought into her suitcase.

"What's wrong?" Max asks concern.

"I cannot find my black shirt with the glitter on the front of it or my pink New York Hoody." Sarah sighed with confusion.

"Awe baby you must have left it in the trunk of the car. I will buy you a new one." Max proclaimed caressing Sarah's back.

They laid down as tomorrow was approaching quickly. Sarah had a five a.m. flight and Max had to be at work at six a.m.

After a long strange day yesterday it was time for Sarah to get home.

Sarah stared at Max as he slept. The alarm went off promptly at four a.m. She silenced the alarm and continued to stare at Max as he laid undisturbed by the alarm clock. Sarah stroked Max's face with the tip of her fingers.

Max moaned and rolled over, pulling the covers over his head. Sarah yanked the covers off Max and proceed to kiss him all over his face. He squirmed trying to avoid Sarah's morning breath. He rolled over on Sarah and tickled her until she begged him to stop. They embraced each other's presence for the last time before getting ready. The taxi driver called Sarah cell informing her that he was outside waiting to drop her off at the airport. Max walked Sarah down to the cab.

"I'm going to miss you," Max said. He kissed Sarah's neck and squeezed her.

"I'm going to miss you too, Lil Daddy. As always, be safe and have a blessed day. I love you much."

Max shut the cab door.

Sarah felt that leaving him was never a problem-- knowing he was not going to be there was. Sarah checked her bags in and boarded the plane to Saint Louis. She still had not overcome her fear of flying, so when instructed by the flight attended to turn on electronics, she put on her headphones and drifted off. Sarah was not feeling well. Her stomach was in a knot. Something was wrong, but she didn't know what, and she couldn't shake the feeling. An unfamiliar car was parked outside their house when she arrived home. Sarah called Max several times for hours but did not receive an answer. She walked swiftly around the house looking into every window. From a distance, she heard a very stimulating man's voice.

"Hey baby, I'll be in there in a minute," said the man.
"Ok, baby hurry up." the woman smiled.

Loud footsteps echoed throughout the house and ceased. The man had come into the room commanding the woman in an unlawful manner. Not in disbelief, but hurt and heartbroken, Sarah crept into the back door of their house. She tip-toed to the stove and turned the oven to broil at five hundred degrees and placed a pan with old cooking grease that was filled three inches from the rim into the oven. Sarah ran back to her truck, barely closing the door. She drove off in tears. She swore her tears spoke to her saying, "I told you so," as they exited her eyes and caressed her cheek.

Sarah's phone rang.

"Hello, Hello, Sarah are you there?" The woman was hysterical.

"Yes, I'm here. May I asked who this is?" Sarah felt uneasy.

"Johnnie May from next door." The woman was out of breath.

"Child, I's was calling to tell you that your house was on fire. The fire department here now, but the ambulance took somebody away I thought it was you or maybe your husband. I know the kids at school. So I know it wasn't nah one of them."

"Hey, Ms. Johnny Mae I have to take this call. Thanks for calling me."

The hospital informed Sarah about Max's arrival. After receiving a call about Max, Sarah became dumbfounded visualizing what she saw, trying to justify what she did was the best thing to do. She didn't rush to the hospital; instead, she waited several hours before arriving, hoping visitation hours were over. She made it obvious that Max was collateral damage. Upon arrival at the hospital, Sarah was escorted to Max's room where he laid sleeping in the hospital bed. He had bandages all over his body, including his face. A sense of revenge bargained with Sarah while she stood over him with a throbbing headache and eyes swollen from weeping for hours. She wanted to console him, but she was inflamed with anger that was not going away anytime soon. She felt horrible for doing this to him, but she also felt pleased because he got what he deserved. She stepped out his room and approached his nurse who was sitting at the desk. Sarah enhanced her worries for Max welfare; however, her concerns were geared more towards if anyone else was brought in with him.

"How is he doing?" Sarah asked the nurse in a d

"He's doing well, and to answer your question

alone," the nurse said looking down at her chart.

Sarah felt a little relieved yet still disappointed. She scratched being the talk of the town off her list of worries.

"The fireman told me that he search the house after they put out the fire. It was an oven fire. It appears your husband may have just fallen asleep. He may have tried to preheat the oven without checking inside the oven to insure there was nothing inside. Your neighbor is the person who called and informed the station of the fire. He's a very lucky man to still be alive. It could have been worst. If there is nothing else I can help you with, Mrs. Houston, I have to finish my rounds before my shift is over."

"No. Thank you." Sarah smiled weakly.

"Ok." The nurse nodded before walking off.

Sarah went back into Max's room and sat beside him. She couldn't even look at him. She was hurting so bad. She began to pray and cry out to God.

There was a sound bounce followed by a long beeping sound. "Excuse me, miss, excuse me, the plane has landed, and you can now leave the plane."

Sarah rubbed her eyes and realized that she had dozed off.

"Thank you," she said quietly.

Sarah grabbed her purse from the overhead storage and headed to baggage claim.

Weeks had gone by. Max had not been successful at getting his car out of the tow yard. He called Sarah with a sense of hope. He only asks for her help when his pride takes a leave of absence. He told Sarah that the towing company will release the car if he gets it registered. Sarah knew getting the car registered would be complicated and very expensive. It's been two and a half years since Max purchase the car. Sarah realized she had to act fast; twelve days had already passed. They had three more days before the tow company proceeded to auction Max's car off or call the car dealership Max got the car from and tell them to come get the car. She worked diligently to get

Max's car registered. She succeeded after paying $1,985. She was told by the license bureau that he missed the end of year deadline. Therefore, three months from now, he would have to pay $500 more to renew his plates.

The next day Sarah flew to New York. She had arrived at the tow company before it closed for the weekend. She showed the tow company that she registered the car and told them she came prepared to pay the seven hundred fifty dollar fine that was placed on the car while it sat in the tow yard. The manager informed Sarah that the dealership came and got the car yesterday. When she heard the news, her stomach dropped and butterflies immediately took over her stomach, pushing back her internal organs. She feared this would not go over well with Max. He was upset when she told him. He called the dealership, and they directed him to the investment company. The finance company reported that he would have to pay $1,750 to get the car back. Max sent the company the money through Western Union. He was then told by the company after he sent the money that he had to reapply for a loan. This was not good at all. Even though Max made decent wages, it wasn't sufficient, he wasn't on his current job long enough. They informed him that if he wanted to keep the car he would have to pay $450 instead of $299 a month. He still had a balance of $14,545 on the car. Sarah and Max agreed it would be best if Max let the car stay at the dealership. They still had two other vehicles that functioned perfectly, even though this would have been a total of two vehicles they allowed to go back to the dealership (Sarah's truck and now Max's car.)

A month later, the dealership sent a letter informing Max that they auction off his old car. They claim to have only gotten $4,540. Max was responsible for paying the remaining balance of $10,005. They gave him thirty days to pay it back. Their sense of financial freedom had flat-lined. They pushed so hard to get out of debt. They felt they were finally at a point in their life where they could enjoy the extra money that was coming in. Max felt as if his working was in vain. Sarah, however, knew that they had accomplished a lot since she helped Max get out of debt. Their house was no longer in foreclosure status; they bought a new seasonal house in Mississippi, and they paid off the title loan they had on his truck.

Max's days of living the fast life in the crowded, busy city that never sleeps had come to a halt. He made the mind-boggling decision to walk away from his dream job to be with his family. He made it home just before Thanksgiving. Max shared his feelings and concerns about Hannah and Haven's surroundings. He wanted to raise the girls in a quiet and slow paced environment, Mississippi perhaps. Sarah never had in her twenty-five years been to Mississippi other than to visit Max's family. She couldn't see herself leaving her family, friends, and church.

Oh, What would I do without a church home? I need balance, Sarah thought to herself.

She realized at the end of the day because Max has done so much for her and the girls, the least she could do was try it. Max sat on the couch in the living room watching TV. Sarah came in the room and sat down beside him. Sarah laid her head in his lap and looked up at him smiling.

"What's up babe?" Max asked pushing her hair back from her face.

He glanced at Sarah and continued to watch TV. She wasn't expecting to have all of his attention. That would have been too much for him to handle since he was watching "Sports Center" for the fiftieth time today.

"I have been thinking. You said you wanted to go to Mississippi, right?"

"Yes," Max responded, "That would be nice. I want to get away from all this crime. Do you know what I mean?" He stroked her cheek.

Sarah hated when he said that: (do you know what I mean).

Sarah was sure that's his way of misleading you in a conversation. After he says, 'Do you know what I mean', you're unknowingly, automatically saying yes, even if you didn't hear what he said or if you agree with what he just said. Sarah just smiled.

She thought to herself. *I grew up in Saint Louis; it's always been bad. Heck, I grew up in the hood. Around ran down houses, drug addicts, drug dealers, thieves, prostitutes, etc. Whatever has happened before will happen again. Whatever has been done before will be done again. There is nothing new under the sun. That's the reason I bought this house in the county when I turned twenty-one. I refuse to have Hannah around the madness even though I turned out fine. At least that's what they keep telling me, I sometimes think different.* Sarah often pondered on what Bishop Edwards said in his sermon, "can anything good come from the hood."

Sarah wanted to tell Max what she was thinking, but she did not. She knew he wouldn't understand her passion for not wanting to forget where she came from even though she fought so hard to get away. She believed her surroundings help mold her to the woman she had become. She realized she wouldn't be as independently sound without it. Max was snobby when it came to the hood or in his words low class, no manners, lazy people with the inability to get a real career. He said they sold drugs or their body in exchange for money. Sarah thought to herself. *Max haven't seen my hood side. Although not many people have. I keep my circle of friends small. I've learned to adjust to my surroundings, yet never losing sight of who I am.*

Max was only familiar with Sarah being quiet, smart, sophisticated, spoiled to perfection, conservative, saved and very girly, so she saw it necessary to keep it that way. "How long were you planning on staying down there?" Sarah asked Max.

"Umm, I'm not sure. Why did you ask me that? I would say until we save some money. I can go back to New York and work for a while. It won't take long for us to save some money if we move to Mississippi. We won't have half the bills we have here. The only thing we would have to pay there is water, lights, mortgage, and trash. Whereas here in Saint Louis, we have to pay water, sewer, trash, gas, electric, personal property taxes along with a whole lot of bull crap." said Max.

"I was going to say we can move down there for a little while and come back to Saint Louis?"

"What? Are you serious?" Max smiled as he jumped up from off the couch with excitement.

"Yes, but only for a little while. Be advised that I will be coming back to Saint Louis at least once a month. Remember, we can't stay down there for good. Most importantly you cannot travel and work while I'm down there. I don't want to be in a state where I don't know anyone."

"You know my family. Baby, you don't have to worry about me working anywhere else other than Mississippi. I heard they have a lot of work there; I'll call the job line in the morning and line some stuff up."

"No. Well, I know them, but not like I know my family. That sounds good."

"Oh, baby thank you, thank you! I love you so much." Max kissed Sarah all over her face.

"So when do we leave?"

"When do you want to leave, I'll leave it up to you." Max smiled.

"I guess two weeks from now. I'll have to let my boss know that I'll be leaving. The kids will be on winter break. That would be perfect. That will give me enough time to get the kids' school transfer papers so I can enroll them in school down there."

"Ok, that sounds good baby doll. I'm so happy about you changing your mind." Max smiled and proceeded to watch "Sports Center".

CHAPTER EIGHT

Moving day came sooner than Sarah anticipated. She had attended Sunday service for the last time before she moved to Mississippi. She stopped by Bishop Edwards's office after church.

"Hey, Bishop Edwards." Sarah knocked on his office door before entering.

"Come in. Hey daughter, I hear you leaving us. Now I have to find someone else to give me a manicure and pedicure." He chuckled.

"Yeah," Sarah said in a sad tone. "I'm sorry, Bishop. I will make sure I take care of your nails whenever I come visit. I promise."

"How often will that be?"

"Once a month."

"So you want me to wait a full month before I get my nails done?"

"Yes. They should be fine."

"Who in their right mind would do that? Not I. I am not about to wait a whole month! You got to be crazy." Bishop Edwards looked over at First Lady when he saw her laughing at him.

"Really! Bishop, you have gone longer than that due to your busy schedule. Besides, who else are you going to get to do them other than me? Now you know First Lady not going to do them."

First Lady shook her head along with her hands. She mumbled, "Surely not I." She laughed looking down at Bishop's feet, scrunching up her face.

Not that he had bad feet but because she preferred not to do them.

113

"Hold up now, daughter. Don't you get sassy with me!" He laughed, bumping Sarah slightly on her arm.

"First Lady and I told you this was coming, didn't we?"

"Yes, you did, but I didn't want to believe it. I remember saying if he tried to move us, I wouldn't go. I'll be sitting in church every Sunday as nothing happened." Sarah laughed.

"Yeah, we hate to see you go, but you know you have to follow your husband. Remember, as long as you all keep God first, each other second, stay prayed up, and put on the full armor of God daily, you will be all right. When you get settled in Mississippi, God will lead you to a church because he places all his members in the church. Until God places you, you remember you are a church; your foundation has already been laid. Don't be afraid of what's to come, daughter, because God has equipped you for such a time as this." Bishop Edwards just smiled. "I love you, daughter. Keep in touch."

"I will." Sarah hugged Bishop Edwards and First Lady Edwards before leaving Bishop Edwards' office.

Sarah arrived at their house and found that their entire house had been packed up and loaded onto the U-Haul truck. She was confused and slightly upset.

Max said that he wanted to leave the things they loaded onto a truck in Mississippi. He promised that when they move back to Saint Louis, he will replace the old furniture by buying new furniture. Sarah knew when Max was stirring off course, overriding their agreement. She soon realized that her nightmare was coming true right before her eyes, and it was impossible for her to smack herself to wake up. They were moving to Mississippi with no intent of returning to Saint Louis, other than to visit. Max's promise of staying in Mississippi for six months and Saint Louis for six months was like words never have been spoken.

Max and their two dogs road in the U-Haul while Haven, Hannah, Sarah and her mom traveled behind Max in their truck. Sarah's drive was filled with disappointment followed by her angry mother's opinions on why Sarah allowed Max to move her so far away from her mother. Eight hours later, they arrived at their house in Mississippi. It wasn't long before her mom began to ridicule everything that caught her eye.

"Sarah is this your first time seeing this house?" Sarah's mom scoffed.

"No, Mom, I have been here several times," Sarah said feeling annoyed.

"Well, common sense should have told your butt, and I know it did, not to move out here. Where in the world are the neighbors? You are in the middle of nowhere! I haven't even seen a person. Oh, there go one," she said shaking her head. She was referring to a car driving by their house. "Ain't no telling when you will see another person."

Sarah gave her mother a blank stare of disdain and continued to unload their clothes from the truck, putting them into the house.

"There is nothing here in this desert. I mean, it looks like they just started cutting down trees and building stuff," said Sarah's mom.

"That's anywhere you go in the world, Mom. Mississippi just doesn't have many buildings here," Sarah explained as she refrained from blowing her top.

"I see. That's okay because I won't be back; I came, I saw, now I will be going." She said in a disturbing tone.
How could she say such a thing? Some things never change, Sarah thought to herself. Sarah shook her head and hid her feelings of abandonment.

Once everyone got settled, Sarah cooked dinner. Everyone sat at the table and ate quietly. There was a sort of tension between Sarah and her mother. Sarah knew it was because her mother was angry with Sarah leaving Saint Louis. Sarah's mom got up and cleared her plate after she finished eating.

"Thanks for dinner Sarah." Sarah's mom said smugly. "You could have put a little more seasoning on that chicken."

She walked into their guest bedroom to go to sleep.

"Mom, can I have a hug?" said Hannah.

"Sure sweetheart." Sarah stooped over to give Hannah a hug. "Mmmuah." Hannah kissed Sarah on the cheek. "I love you, Momma," said Hannah.

"I love you to double H." Sarah said smiling at Hannah.

"Hey, Mom, the food was great, and the chicken was finger licking good. Granny can be mean and rude sometimes. We have to keep praying for her, ain't that right momma?"

"Yes sweetie." Sarah nodded her head in agreement.

Hannah joined Haven in their bedroom and prepared to go to sleep.

"I am exhausted," Sarah said falling face first down into their comforter.

Max rubbed Sarah's back until her eyelids surrendered and shut down for the night.

"Mommy!" Haven called. "Daddy." Haven rolled out of bed. She shivered as she walked throughout the dark, frozen, house. She approached the front door in efforts to open it. She had struggled a bit before she was successful.

Sarah became parched while sleeping. "Ugh, I can never sleep the entire night without getting cotton mouth," said Sarah. She put on her robe and dragged her feet throughout the hallway headed toward the kitchen.

"What the....," said Sarah. She forced herself to focus.

"Who left this door wide open?" Sarah said. She walked onto the porch and looked around, but didn't see anything or anyone. "Don't tell me we have to get a new door," Sarah groaned quietly. She shook her head with disappointment. Sarah thought of the girls and immediately ran to check on them. Hannah was still sleeping; however, Haven wasn't in her bed.

Sarah ran throughout the house looking for Haven; there was no sign of her. She ran outside looking for her; she looked into the street at the pile of clothes she glanced at before going back into the house earlier. She jogged barefoot toward the clothes. The closer she got, the more she could hear,

"Mommy, the truck didn't stop."

"Awe, Lord not my baby, my precious baby." Sarah cried out uncontrollably.

"Mrs. Houston we regret to inform you but we couldn't save your daughter."

"Why, why Lord!" Sarah shouted in agonizing pain.
The Lord spoke to her, "I didn't do this Sarah, the enemy comes to kill, steal and destroy, and I come so that you may have life and that more abundantly." His voice faded.
"Aww, he took my baby from me!" Sarah said, kicking and screaming. "No!"

"Baby! Baby, wake up, wake up! You're dreaming," Max shouted in Sarah's ear as he attempted to wake her.
"Where are the girls?" Sarah demanded with confusion and desperation as tears swam down her face onto her shirt that was already consumed in sweat.
"They're in their room sleep."
"How do you know?" Sarah asked.
"Because you put them to bed right before we laid down together, baby; you were sleep only for about ten minutes."
"I have to go check on them," Sarah said, crawling out of bed.
Boom!
Sarah fell onto the floor as she fought the covers that were holding her back.

"Baby, are you alright?" Max asked, helping Sarah off the floor.

"Yes, I tripped over this stupid cover." Sarah rushed to the girl's bedroom. Hannah and Haven were sound asleep tucked comfortably in their cozy bed.

"Oh my God, Max! I just had a horrible dream, I was sleeping and Haven got up and went outside. She ran out into the streets and got hit by a truck. I saw her laying there. It reminded me of the movie *Pet Cemetery* when the little boy got hit by that truck." Sarah closed her eyes and put her head down. She trembled at the thought that something like that could happen.

Max put his arm around Sarah, pulling her close to him. "Where was I? Was I in your dream?"

Sarah looked up at Max for a brief second before dropping her head again. She shook her head. "No, you weren't there, and I don't remember crying out for you or anything." Sarah started to cry.

"Baby, it's going to be all right. It was just a dream; nothing like that is going to happen to Haven or Hannah. You are a great mother. You never let them out of your sight, so you have no reason to worry. God is in control."

Max kissed her on the forehead. "I love you, baby doll."

"I love you too, Lil Daddy." Sarah laid her head firmly on Max's chest. She went to sleep as he held her securely in his arms.

It had been three weeks since the big move. Max hadn't been successful at finding a job; it turns out the work site he had in mind didn't start until the end of February. That was a month away. Max became cranky and very hard to live with; their funds were getting low, not to mention they still had to take Sarah's mom back home.

Monday morning, Max received a phone call.

"Hello, yes this is he." Max sat up in the bed.

"No sir, I'm not working. Yes sir, I can be there in the morning." Said Max.

Sarah quickly turned and looked at Max as she laid in the bed. "Who was that?" Sarah asked with curiosity.

"A job," Max replied aggressively.

"Ok, where is it? I heard you say you will be there tomorrow." Sarah thoughts hovered waiting on Max's respond.

"It's in Memphis," Max said with an attitude that Sarah certainly didn't tolerate.

"What?! In Memphis!" Sarah said, raising her voice as she angered. "Now why would you take that job? We agreed that if I moved down here that you wouldn't travel anymore."

"Well, what else you want me to do? We will lose

everything if I don't go to work. Did you develop amnesia overnight or something? We have to take your mom back home. How are we going to do that without any money? Besides that, it's only for four days, 12-hour shifts. Do you think your mom will stay here until I come back?" Max said, looking desperate.

"I don't know! Heck I don't know if I want to stay until you get back." Sarah shook my head with disappointment. "You talk to her; I'm not asking her to do anything. I don't want to hear her mouth."

"Ok, I will," Max replied as he stood to put on his pants he had on yesterday.

"Max do you have any idea why I'm so mad?" Sarah folded her arms.

"Why?" He responded nonchalantly. He put on his shirt.

"Because you still doing the same stupid stuff. You get a job and tell me about it later. You said we were only moving down here for a little while, and the next thing I know, you packed the entire house. Now I have to rent the house out in Saint Louis. I worked so hard to get it and keep it; therefore, I refuse to lose it. Then you accepted that job all the way in Memphis! That's like three hours from here, if not longer. What was crazy on your part was that you neglected to talk it over with me, which hurt. I am your wife Max, not your psycho ex-girlfriend, your booty call, or fantasy girl. We are no longer dating. We are married! It would be nice if you start acting like it and run your life changing events by me first."

Sarah struggled to keep her hands to herself. Max sensed a touch of Sarah's rage, and he regrouped. "I know baby. I'm sorry. I will do better, but Memphis is not too far from here, I wouldn't go if we didn't need the money. You know that just as well as I do, this will be the last time. I promise." Max gave her a hug and kiss on the forehead.

"How else I'm I going to be able to afford to keep my beautiful wife happy? I'm going to miss you," said Max.

"I know I'm going to miss you too. Hurry up and come back. I can't stand to be a prisoner in my home. Oh, and just to let you know, you still have to ask your mother-in- law if she would stay here while you go out of town."

"Come on baby! Can you ask her, please?" Max gave Sarah a face only a mother could love.

She shook her head. "No. You're the one leaving; plus, you will have a better chance at asking her then I would. You know she likes you better than me."

"She does, doesn't she?" Max smiled.

"Hey Max," Sarah whispered.

"What's up baby?"

"Word in the sheets, is you got that one hitta quitta." Sarah smiled at Max with her eyes.

"So, what you're saying is you want to find out." Max loosened his smile. "Wait your mom is here."

"Okay, so what does that mean?" Sarah said, feeling anxious.

"She can hear us."

"I'll be quiet I promise; it's you who I'm worried about. She knows we don't own any baby sheep." Sarah laughed.

"Ok, we have to hurry before the kids get up."

"I'm on it." Here you are going to need this, Sarah tried stuffing Max's mouth with a towel.

"What are you doing?" Max moved his head from side to side, so Sarah couldn't muzzle him.

"You said we had to keep down the noise, so I figured if I stuff your mouth, it will be nice and quiet then." Sarah chuckled.

"Really? I think you have me confused with yourself." Max then gave Sarah specific instructions.

Sarah felt it was mandatory that she and Max had a sense of connection before he left to go out of town. It gave her a sense of security.

Max departed to Memphis while Sarah, her mother, and the girls stayed home. Sure enough, when the four days were over, Max came home. The next day, they wasted no time driving Sarah's mom back to Saint Louis. *Yes! I am no longer a prisoner in my home.* Sarah paused for a moment to celebrate her being free in her mind.

Max and Sarah worked diligently on their house in St. Louis. They painted the interior, replaced the carpet in two of the main floor bedrooms and shampooed the other rooms, replaced blinds and made sure the outside of the house was up to part. Sarah placed "For Rent" ads in the newspaper and on free social media sites once the house became available to rent; it wasn't long before they found a tenant. Sadly, Sarah's monthly mortgage payment went from five hundred thirty-five dollars to seven hundred ninety-five dollars within the past few years. As a result, Sarah had to charge eight hundred dollars a month for rent. She wasn't making a profit. However, she felt blessed to be able to keep her house. Somehow, somewhere down the line, they fell behind in their mortgage payments, forcing the bank to foreclose on their house. Luckily, a friend of Sarah's filed for bankruptcy and was able to walk Sarah through the process. She explained to Sarah that if she filed a chapter thirteen she could keep her house, so she did just that. She was able to consolidate all her debt into one monthly payment that she had to send to the trustee's office. Sarah sent a separate payment to her mortgage-company.

CHAPTER NINE

Max found himself back on the stumbling block when they returned to Mississippi: he couldn't find a job. They had not saved any money from him previously working; this has become a miserable trend. They had ran low on their financial resources. Max went into most of his annuity accounts; however, the accounts that had an extractable balance wasn't perceptible because all their bills were paid, and they weren't at risk of losing anything. He couldn't file unemployment because he owed the unemployment office over $4,000. Consequently, when he found a job a while back, he failed to inform the unemployment office that he was working. He reported he was unemployed three times before he told the unemployment office he had gained employment; he figured it was his money. They didn't have to worry about food for a while. Sarah's mother blessed them with over three hundred dollars' worth of groceries before they took her back to Saint Louis. Several members of Max's family invited them over for dinner every night. They ensured that Sarah felt like a part of the family.

Every morning, Max went to the union hall in Jackson, Mississippi in hopes to get a job near their house. While leaving the union hall, Max called Sarah.

"Hey baby, what are you doing?" Max asked.

"Nothing. I'm watching TV. I don't feel too good. My stomach is hurting," Sarah sighed. She caressed her stomach in hopes to sooth the pain.

"Uh, what do you think about going to Florida?"

"That sounds great! When?"

"I'm not sure, maybe now would be a good time."

"In January, really? Do you think it's going to be hot around this time of year?" Sarah was unsure about Max's date.

"Of course! Did you forget I use to stay in Florida? It doesn't get frigid there. However, it does get nippy at night. I'll talk to you when I make it home; I'm headed that way now."

Max hung up the phone.

Max walked in the house with a smirk on his face thirty minutes later. He walked past Sarah going into the kitchen, putting his car keys on the key hanger. He then pulled a chair from the kitchen rolling it into the front room where Sarah was sitting. He sat in front of her while she sat on the couch watching TV.

"Hey babe, guess what?" said Max.

"What?" Sarah said, looking at Max. She knew he was up to something.

"Do you remember when I asked you if you wanted to go to Florida," Max smiled.

"Yes." Sarah thought to myself. Now I know this fool better not say he is going to work in Florida.

"Well, today two people called me about a job, Florida and Texas. I told them that I had to talk it over with my wife first before I made a decision." Max tried charming Sarah with his irresistible smile. Sarah knew he had already predetermined where he wanted to work.

"So, which state would you like to visit, Florida or Texas? Whichever one you choose that's the state I will accept."

"What?" Sarah said quickly. *This ninja has lost his mind completely,* she thought to herself while exposing her deepest emotions through her face.

"Nan one! Both of those places are far away," Sarah protested trying to control her anger.

"But baby those are the only jobs hiring right now." Max tried convincing Sarah the best way he knew how. "You already know I have to go wherever the work is. If I don't work, we will lose our insurance. Listen to yourself. You're complaining about your stomach now. What if you have to go to the doctor? Here in Mississippi, if you don't have insurance, you have to pay with cash or check up front. If you can't afford to do that, the nurse won't admit you, and then you have to go to the emergency room; they will accept you, but they are going to tax you. That's an extra expense we don't need. All I'm saying is that we don't need to lose our insurance because it will take a while for me to get it back," Max argued.

Sarah looked at Max and shook her head. *What in the world does this dude take me for,* Sarah asked herself.

Max became upset. It was obvious; he wasn't happy with the direction their conversation was headed. He aggressively got up out of the chair pushing it slightly and walked outside slamming the door behind him.

Sarah groaned. *I hate that he acts like a big ole baby sometimes. Who am I fooling? He acts like that all the dang gone time. Then I'm left to play momma and fix the problem he created; that's so not fair,"* Sarah pouted and took a deep soothing breath. *What was he thinking, asking me to allow him to go so far away and work? Based on his reaction, he couldn't have thought about it long enough.*

"Ugh!" Sarah yelled in an untamable tone. She began to pray. "Lord! I don't know what to do. I know we need the money, but I don't want him to go. It seems like he just came back home, and sadly enough he's trying to leave again. I don't get him. He claims he's so happy with our relationship but he's always so eager to jump ship when given the opportunity. What did I do? I can't believe I gave up my independent worry-free life for this," Sarah sighed refusing to cry.

While sitting in silence, she heard God say, "Let him go. I will protect you." Sarah felt unruffled as his soft, pleasant voice was very reassuring. She took a minute to reevaluate the situation only to find herself wanting to do the opposite of what God told her to do.

She rationalized a bit more. "I know obedience is better than sacrifice, but being obedient feels as though it is beyond my reach, and telling him he couldn't go was one sacrifice I'm willing to make. Lord, I have no clue as to why I should let him go, but I trust you; you said, you'll never leave me nor forsake me," Sarah said. She picked up her cell phone from in between the couch pillows. She repentantly text Max.

"Ok, I thought long and hard about it. I decided it is ok for you to go. You better thank God that I love you."

Max ran back into the house barely closing the front door behind him. He ran over to Sarah and picked her up from off the couch. He kissed her all over her face as she squirmed trying to get away from him. Max loved kissing Sarah all over her face. He knew she hated when he did that. If Max wasn't working, he wasn't living. Sarah knew it would have been foolish of her to knock his drive of wanting to work so he could provide for her, Hannah, and Haven.

"Well, I have to say that I appreciate you running your job offers by me first. So when do you leave," Sarah asked Max.

"Well, it's a 13-hour drive from here, I think. I'm not one hundred percent sure; I need you to look up the directions for me. I have to leave out the house no later than four a.m. tomorrow morning," Max explained.

Max departed as he said he would. He arrived in Florida thirteen hours later. He called Sarah once he arrived at the Union Hall in Florida.

"Hey baby doll. How is everything going?"

"It's going well. I just finish reading our girls a bedtime story." "How is my man of steel doing?"

Max laughed loudly, "I'm doing great baby, just a little tired. The Union Hall is closed for today. I'm an hour ahead of you, so I'm going to lay back in my truck and go to sleep. I want to be well rested for tomorrow. I have to take a test before I get hired for the job. I will get paid while I'm here testing. They may just put me to work. I hear they have been putting a lot of guys to work as soon as they arrive, but no matter how good you work, if you fail that test you have to go home, and you can't take it again for ninety days."

"Ok, Lil Daddy. I'm going to let you go to sleep. I love you more than you will ever know."

"I love you too baby doll. Hugs and kisses; give me a kiss."

"Mahwah, goodnight."

While Max was preparing for his test in Florida, Sarah was having a test of her own back in Mississippi. The thoughts of her husband being miles away from her and her family being beyond arms' reach has been planted in her mind and were weighing heavily on her. She refuses to tell her parents that Max is out of town working again because she knows they would be very upset that Max would leave his family home alone in the wilderness as Sarah's mother would say. When Sarah talked to her parents, they would always ask her, "Where's Max?" she would say, "He's at work." She figured she wasn't lying; he has been at work, just in another state, which was 13 hours away. God forbid if something were to happen to her or the girls, it would take a while for Max to reach them. The only thing that was keeping Sarah from going insane was church.

Sarah, Max, and their girls have been going to Max's cousin church every Sunday since they determined the other churches wasn't working for them. The first day Sarah visited this Pentecostal, Holy Spirit-filled church, she immediately felt God's presence when she walked through the door. It reminded her so much of their church back home minus the greeters at the front entry way giving warm hugs and a bright, welcoming smile that would turn any frown upside down. Besides all the negative feedback she was receiving from others about this church, she knew God had placed her there. She attended noon day Bible study every Tuesday; she never missed. She felt that she had no reason to. There was still so much she had to learn about God and the plans he had for her, along with the steps she needed to take to get there.

Therefore, she studied to show herself approved. Her land was broken. Every time she turned around there was a different part of her life sinking like quicksand. Max was gone; the girls began to misbehave in school; she wasn't feeling her best. She was weak all the time and sick to her stomach. She lost ten pounds. She had bad body cramps and migraines that felt like atomic bombs going off every five minutes; Tylenol and Sarah became very close; she couldn't make it through the day without a capsule or two. She needed God to heal her land, and she knew that if she just focus on Him, He will. She believes He will keep her sane in an insane situation.

A month had passed, and still no sign of Max. Sarah had gotten to the point where she didn't care how she looked. She went from dressing up every day looking cute for Max to looking like somebody's neglected Barbie whose hair has been cut into patches. She deprived herself of everything she once knew. She didn't attempt to do her hair. She kept it in a ponytail that became nappy over time because she never combed it. She eventually stop talking to friends and family. Oftentimes, when she heard Max's voice she would get angry. She would find a reason to get off the phone with him so she wouldn't lash out on him.

"Hey, baby I miss you. I wish I could see you." The message rolled across Sarah phone Saturday night; this caused Sarah to explode emotionally and mentally.
Sarah became furious wondering how he could fix his lips to say that, and she sent him a lengthy, enraged text message.
"You say you love me, and you miss me, but I haven't seen you in two months. I barely talk to you. The kids miss you. They keep asking me when you are coming home. I don't want to go through the same thing as before. I need you here with me. Max I'm hurting. Something is wrong with me. I can't sleep because I'm afraid. I'm afraid someone is going to break into the house, and no one would hear us scream out for help because we are in the middle of nowhere. I turn on all the lights in the house at night. I keep having nightmares about wild animals. The devil is taking over the thoughts that I have of you, and he's twisting them. He's tormenting me like never before. I'm lonely. I'm starting to question why we get married. I'm hurting Max, can't you tell. I've lost ten pounds if not more since you've been gone. Why would you bring me down here and leave me? It's not fair to me."
She cried like a baby as she express her feelings to Max via text. "You said your family would be here for me. They haven't been by to see me, neither have they called. I stop

talking to your sister because it seems like she was always trying to break us up. She would say things like, girl you better than me. I would have been left that ninja if he did me like that. You a good one. She would also say things like she hates talking to you because you were always bragging about what you have--that you think you better than everybody else. Even though I know you're not like that anymore, I don't want to hear that mess. I need you Max; I need my husband, and the girls need their dad. I hate to say this but if you want to continue to travel you're going to have to do it without me. I'm moving back to Saint Louis, so don't be surprised if I'm gone when you get back."

"Ok, I understand." Max responded. He tried to register what he thought, but he was speechless. Sarah's bipolar behavior was taking charge.

Sarah sat on the bedroom floor and cried out to God until she fell asleep. Sunday morning, she woke up still lying on the bedroom floor, debating if she wanted to go to church or not. Since she was saved, this was something she probably did twice. There was a knock at her bedroom door.

"Who is it?" Sarah said in a pleasant tone.

"It's me, Momma," said Hannah. "Can I come in?"

"Yes, baby."

Hannah walked into the bedroom holding Haven by the hand. They both were smiling.

"Hey Mom", said Haven. We wanted to go to Sunday school. We wanted to let you know we were ready. Do you think we're going to make it in time?"

"What time is it Haven?" Sarah asked.

"It's nine hundred thirty-one," said Haven looking at the digital clock on the night stand.

Hannah and Sarah laughed. "You mean nine thirty-one," said Hannah, correcting Haven as she does everyone.

"I helped Haven get dressed," said Hannah. "Can we have some cereal? I can make it so you can take your time getting dressed for church."

"Sure. You guys look gorgeous. Make sure you don't mess

up your clothes. Put a bath towel around Haven just to be safe."

"Momma, remember Sunday school starts at ten o'clock a.m. It takes us twenty minutes to get to church."

"I am very aware of this, Hannah, go eat. I'll be ready shortly." "That little girl of mine reminds me why I prefer not to have another girl every time she opens her mouth to say something smart. When she does, I always remember my mother saying, 'if you ever have children, they are going to do everything you did as a child.' I wish I would have listened. Although I don't recall ever talking back or getting smart with an adult like Hannah tends to do at times. Maybe because my mother would have ripped my tongue out as soon as I did." Sarah said to herself after the girls went into the kitchen.

Sarah stood up from off the floor. She opened the door to their walk-in closet. It appeared it had been hit by a tornado: clothes and shoes were everywhere. She could easily remove the word walk in from walk-in closet and just say closet. She couldn't step foot into it. She have not cleaned it since Max left. Surely if Max saw this closet he would freak out since he's such a neat freak. Everything has to be nice and ship-shape, including her, so she makes sure she's dolled up when Max comes home from work or when she goes out in public. She does it for herself just as well as him. It makes her happy knowing she made him happy. What woman doesn't want to make her husband happy? Although, sometimes she feels like an expensive Barbie doll placed on display, especially around Max's friends and family. She could hear him saying, "Baby stop slouching. Can you sit up straight? Baby, don't eat that instead eat this. Can you put on a belt (even though her pants fit perfect, and she don't need one). I don't like those pants; throw them away. I'll replace them with four new ones. I don't want you to wear fake hair or eyelashes." One day she's Princess Barbie: "Baby you don't have to clean up; I'll do it. You relax," says Max as he catered to her. Then other days she's maid Barbie: "These dishes are not washed right. They still have grease on them; they don't even look clean. Please don't fold my clothes if you can't fold them the way that I like them. I work hard and have to come home to a nasty house (but the house is clean. Hannah didn't take out the trash)." Sarah gets irked at the fact he's always complains about something; he can be happy one minute than mad the next because of something stupid like she bought an off-brand ketchup vs. Heinz ketchup.

When Max goes out of town, Sarah feels the need to take a break from being Cinderella. She clean when she wants to, she refrains from getting all dolled up, and she wear jeans, jogging pants, and tights. But as soon as he makes the call or send a text saying, "Baby I'm on my way home", then it's crunch time for Sarah, Hannah, and Haven. They'll be cooking, cleaning, wiping down walls, and scrubbing floors. Sarah tries her best to keep the house clean when Max is away; however, Max and Sarah have two different definitions of clean.

Sarah climbed on top of the mountain of clothes in the closet. She grabbed the first thing she saw, a too little slightly faded black skirt and a dingy black blouse that had a hole on the side of it and underneath the armpit. It was obvious she didn't plan on raising her arms. She wore black tights that had lent balls on them that sadly, she didn't bother with taking them off. She probably should have thrown those clothes away a long time ago. She slipped on her black dress shoes with the worn down heel. They made it to church despite them running late. Sarah dropped the girls off at Sunday school, and she attended the adult Sunday school class across the hall. She couldn't stay focused during the Sunday school lesson due to all the extra baggage she brought with her to church. During praise and worship, Sarah cried out to God.

Pastor Smith got up to preach. "Don't let your situation or circumstance push you out of the presence of God. He knew what you were going to go through before He allowed you to go through it; cast your cares on Him."
Sarah sat talking to God underneath her breath.

"All you have to do is cry out to Him. When you feel like

you can't talk to no one else, know that you can talk to Him, he won't pass judgment on you. He's a great listener and an excellent guidance counselor if you would obey him." Pastor Smith concluded his message saying, "You don't have to worry about Him telling nobody. Everyone standing. Hey Sarah, where's Sister Sarah", Pastor Smith glanced over the crowd looking for her.

Sarah raised her right hand, "Here I am, " she yelled. She stood on her tippy toes so she could be seen from behind the tall couple.

"Sarah sweetheart, come down to the altar. God told me to pray for you." He picked up the bottle of blessing oil and poured a small amount into the palm of his right hand.

Sarah walked desperately down to the altar. When she stood in front of Pastor Smith, she surrendered to God by lifting her hands to the ceiling. Hannah and Haven watched patiently from their seats.

Pastor Smith took the blessing oil and put it on both of her hands before putting it on her forehead in the shape of a cross. He placed his hands on sides of Sarah's head. "Father we come boldly before your throne asking you to watch over Sarah and her family. Lord, she has been so faithful to you. Bring her husband home."

Sarah screamed loudly and began to speak in tongues. Pastor Smith was unaware of Max's absences. Sarah never told him Max was in Florida working.

Pastor Smith continued praying, overriding Sarah's loud voice of utterance. "Lord give her guidance, Lord bless the unborn child in her womb. I cancel any plan of the enemy, Satan take your hands off this family! You can't have them, and they are God's children. Grant her peace and a praying spirit. Lord we will never fail to give you the honor the praise and the glory. In Jesus name, Amen." Pastor Smith hugged, Sarah.

Sarah held her stomach in remembrance of what Pastor Smith had said. She couldn't wrap her mind around the fact that she could be pregnant. This was the second time a man of

God mentioned a child to her. Her biggest concern at the moment was Max, and she didn't want to think of the possibility of her being pregnant at such a horrific time as this. Her phone vibrated shifting her attention long enough for her to bury any sign that she maybe pregnant. After church, Sarah waited until she got home to check her messages. Once she got comfortable, she sat down on the couch and read the text message she received from Max.

"I'm sorry you feel like I haven't been there for you. I'm trying to give my family what I never had. Sometimes I find it hard to be able to provide for my family financially without neglecting them physically. I know it's hard for you to understand my line of work, but you just don't know how I prayed to God asking him to bless me with a job like this. I love you so much. I want to give you and our girls any and everything money can buy. I don't want my family to struggle like I did growing up. Their life is going to be better than ours was growing up. We just have to stick together and keep God first in our lives. He will see to it that all our dreams come to past. You said you wanted a house built from the ground; you want us to start a business together all these things take time and money. With God's help, I can get the money we need; however, it's up to you. I hope you can understand that I have to stay here until I find something close to home. I pray that when that time comes you are at home waiting on me, welcoming me with open arms like you always do."

Sarah smiled and text Max back. "Ok, I understand."

CHAPTER TEN

"Mom-my I have to use the restroom," said Haven. She squirmed in her seat.

"Ok honey wait till they start church announcements," Sarah replied.

"Mom." replied Haven. Haven and Sarah stood up and quickly exited the sanctuary. Pastor Smith was due to approaching the congregation to preach shortly, and Sarah didn't want to miss it. On their way to the bathroom, Sarah looked down at Haven as they talked.

"Oh!"

"Woah," said Sarah. She tried retaining her balance as she was held up. A flirty smile similar to Max's, if not identical, greeted Sarah accompanied by a firm grip of her arm. Sarah smiled back at him. "I am sorry sir. I apologize for stumbling over you. Please forgive me."

The unknown guy continued to smile saying, "Oh it's alright your good, sweetheart."

Sarah smiled and immediately rushed to take Haven to the bathroom as she became impatient and her embarrassment became visible. She realized she had seen this man around town several times. When the kids performed at the church, he would always attend. While waiting on Haven, Sarah stood in the mirror. She began to have unpleasant thoughts about the man. She tried to hide the fact that she was actually blushing. She couldn't brush off the thought of this man: "that guy was fire," Sarah said spontaneously. *I know he has to be....* Sarah thought to herself.

The Holy Spirit began to speak to Sarah: "Wait! Pump your breaks! You are married, and you most definitely shouldn't be thinking or speaking in such a manner. 'Let the words of my mouth, and the meditation of my heart, be acceptable in thy sight'."

Sarah embraced what the Holy Spirit had said. "I shouldn't be thinking like that, but I wonder. I can repent. I know God will forgive me."

The Holy Spirit spoke once more saying, "If anyone, then, knows the good they ought to do and doesn't do it, it is sin for them."

"I couldn't do that to my girls. I would never be able to get away with it; this town is too small." Sarah kept trying to rationalize her feelings. "Okay, Sarah-- it's a sin, crazy girl, Oh yeah. That's right," Sarah laughed to herself. Haven came out of the bathroom stall. She walked over to the sink and washed her hands, and they walked back to the sanctuary. Haven attempted to skip. Sarah squeezed her hand slightly and shook her head no. Haven immediately stopped and walked. The guy she bumped into earlier was still holding up the wall in the foyer. He watched Sarah as she made her way to the sanctuary. Sarah looked straight ahead. She was trying so hard to refrain from looking at Mr. Censored (that's the nickname she gave him). It took Sarah and Haven less than five minutes to get to the bathroom from the sanctuary, but to Sarah it seems to have taken them twice the time making it back. Mr. Censored and Sarah locked eyes. "Dang, Dang it. I almost made it," Sarah said shaking her head. "Lord, don't let this man good looks be the reason you condemn me. Just a few more steps I would have been in the sanctuary, so much for wishful thinking," Sarah said to herself.

They finally made it back to the sanctuary. Pastor Smith was approaching the podium as they sat down. Sarah battled her thoughts as her mind was all over the place. She had a hard time trying to stay focused on what Pastor Smith was saying. Mr. Censored had packed his bags and was moving into her thoughts. She knew she had to get a grip. She focused on bringing her mind into captivity. She began to quote scriptures in her head, "Anyone who looks at another lustfully has already committed adultery with them in their hearts. If a man is found sleeping with another man's wife, both of them must die". Sarah made a pact with her eyes never to look lustfully at another man. "Oh, Lord I need your help, " Sarah screamed underneath her breath, then quickly looked around to see if anyone heard her. Even though she didn't hear anything Pastor Smith preached about, she knew God had her on his mind because the Holy Spirit ministered to her the entire time she sat in church. Upon church dismissal, Sarah gathered the girls and went straight to her truck. She didn't want to stop to talk to anyone. She was afraid of running into Mr. Censored a.k.a Max's long-lost twin. Sarah tapped the remote starter to the truck. She assisted the girls into the truck. Sarah went to the back for their after church snack, a bag of chips and a small juice. She took a quick glance of her surroundings. "No sign of Mr. Censored, " she smiled. She closed the back window and headed back to the front of the truck.

"Hey, how are you doing?" asked a familiar voice coming from behind her, massaging her ear with a pleasant voice.

Sarah turned around quickly only to find that it was the last person she wished to see. "Hey, how are you? I didn't stain your shirt when I bumped into you, did I?" Sarah smiled.

"No, you didn't. I was just admiring you. You are so pretty, and I couldn't let you go without saying something. I wanted to see if we could have dinner as friends," he smiled.

"Sure…… I'm sorry I can't I'm happily married."

"Married!?" he looked puzzled.

"Yes."

"Oh, you didn't have to tell me that ma. That was the first thing I looked for when I first saw you. I saw your ring inside the church. I was asking you about your truck."

Sarah tried offsetting her embarrassment by smiling. She wished she had listened a little closer to what he was saying.

"I said I was just admiring your truck; it's pretty clean given the year. I couldn't let you go without saying something to you about it. That remote starter is nice also."

"Thank you, this is my husband's baby. He's had it for a long time. He takes very good care of it as you can see."

He took a long glance at Sarah then attempted to look at

the truck.

"I love the remote starter especially when it's cold in the morning." said Sarah.

"Ok, sweetheart I don't want to hold you up, I know your man is probably waiting on you." He smiled and mumbled, "I know I would." "It was nice talking to you; I didn't catch your name ma."

"That's because I didn't throw it out to be caught, " Sarah smiled. "My name is Sister Sarah."

"Pretty name. You look like a super model. I know you hear that all the time." He unleashed his flirty smile. "By the way, my name is Marcus," he extended his hand for a handshake. Sarah extended her hand in return.

He grabbed her hand firmly and shook it saying, "It was nice meeting you. I'll be seeing you more often since we go to the same church."

"Likewise." Sarah nodded. She got into the truck and raised her window down. She waited to exit the church parking lot in the line that formed. "Hey, Sister Sarah", yelled Marcus. "Tell your husband if he ever wanted to trade in his baby, I would be more than happy to take her off his hands, " he flashed his flirty smile.

Now I'm almost certain that he wasn't talking about the truck, Sarah thought to herself.

She couldn't wait to tell Lauren, so she texted her.

"Girl you wouldn't believe this. I just committed adultery." Sarah awaited Lauren's reply.

Sarah phone rang.

"Hey girl, can you talk?" asked Lauren when Sarah picked up the phone.

"Yes, the girls are sleeping. I'm driving home."

"So, tell me what happen. How and when did you commit adultery?"

"I committed adultery with my eyes and heart in the church, girl. Who does that?"

"Apparently you. Girl, you are silly. Who was it?"

"Mr. Censored."

"What? That's his name, or is that the name you gave him?" she chuckled.

Sarah laughed. "His name is Marcus, but I call him Mr. Censored because he's too overrated for me. Girl, he looks just like Max. No lie."

"Oh, I see."

"What's crazy is that I see him everywhere at different places. Now he's at the church. I don't think he's committed to going. Sometimes I see him in the foyer more than I do in the sanctuary. That ain't nobody but the devil tempting me," Sarah laughed.

"Really? Sarah, now don't you tell that lie! You know the Bible says, 'But every man is tempted when he is--

"Drawn away of his own lust and enticed, yeah, yeah I know. Then desires become pregnant and gives birth to sin. When sin grows up, it gives birth to death. I can probably quote those scriptures front to back, back to front, but they didn't help me when I bumped into Mr. Censored."

"Those particular scriptures may not have come to you, but I'm sure the Holy Spirit brought something back to your remembrance."

"Yeah, Adultery, Adultery," Sarah laughed. "I was having all kind of wayward thoughts about him. I thought I could cheat just once."

"Naw, that town too small."

"I know right."

"You will be alright. Just pray about it, and ask God to remove those unpleasant thoughts and cast it down when they come, bring them into captivity and make them obey Christ's way of thinking. Where's Max?"

"I don't know."

"Oh, Lord. What happen?"

"Nothing, I'm good. It's nothing I won't get over." Sarah was upset that Max hadn't made it home yet.

"Ok, you need to watch that too. When you and your husband have an argument or not on speaking terms, the enemy knows. He will use that opportunity to crawl through that cracked window; he will make the situation worst. Remember, he knows what we like. Have you made it home yet?"

"Yes"

"Let's pray," suggested Lauren. "Heavenly Father, we come to you as humbly as we know how. You said that when two or three speak of You, there You are in the midst. Lord, I ask that You show your hand in this situation. Please cover my sister-- cleanse and renew her mind and heart of anything that is not of You. We asked that You remove the hand of the enemy. Open the doors of communication between her and her husband. Lord I don't know everything she is going through, but You do. Lord, have her to know that You are in control. We will never fail to give you the honor, the praise, and the glory, in Jesus name, Amen.

"Amen," Sarah wiped the tears from her face. "Thanks, friend. I needed that."

"No problem. I love you. Call me later, once you've gotten the girls settled."

"Ok, I love you too."

Two weeks later Sarah received a call from Max.

"Hey baby doll."

"Hey."

"Well babe, your Lil Daddy coming home. I failed the main test. They said I would have to wait ninety days before I can take it again.

"Yes!" Sarah mumbled. She formed fits and jerked her hand back and forth in excitement. She jumped up from the couch and started dancing. "Thank you Lord," She whispered gleefully. "Awe babe, I'm sorry to hear that," Sarah said, pretending not to be smiling. "Is there anything you want me to do?" She continued to dance.

"No, babe I'm good. I'm just happy that I'm able to come home. This job didn't allow me to take off work."

"Awe, snap. I'm so happy you're coming home. I get to see my Lil daddy," Sarah dance once more. "Aw yeah, Aw yeah, my baby coming home! I said my baby is coming home," Sarah started doing the running man dance by M.C. Hammer followed by Michael Jackson's famous moon walk.

Max laughed, "Are you dancing!"

"And you know this, man!"

"Ok Mami, I'll see you sometime tomorrow. I love you."

"Ok, I love you too. Be safe, and don't leave until you had enough rest."

Sarah immediately called Lauren after getting off the phone with Max to tell her the wonderful news.

"Hello," answered Lauren.

"Girl! Max just called me and said he was coming home tomorrow."

"Praise God! Will he be coming home for good?"

"I don't know yet, as long as he's not working in Florida."

"That's good. How long has it been since he's been gone?"

"Girl, eternity!" Sarah laughed." It's been four months. Please don't remind me." A sense of relief surrounded Sarah.

"What happen? Why is he coming home?"

"He failed one of his tests."

"Wow. I remember you telling me that he has never failed a test for his job before. They let him work that long without letting him take the test first?"

"Well, they had a total of seven tests to take, and it was a lot of people down there working, so it took them awhile to test everyone. The company let them work until they were done taking all of their tests. If they failed any of their tests, they were relieved the same day. They can take the test again after ninety days, but I'm not going to lie: I was praying he failed that test. Call me selfish, but I need my man home."

"Yeah, I feel you on that one."

Sarah stayed up late cooking Max some food for the next day. She didn't want any interruption when Max arrived.

Max made it to Mississippi the next day, after six o'clock p.m. Sarah was in their bedroom taking a nap when she heard a car door shut. She immediately sat up in a panic. Her heart started pounding, and an instant sweat forced its way through her pores. Max walked into the kitchen admiring his favorite dessert sitting on the table. He picked up a brownie and broke a small piece before eating it. "This brownie is hard," said Max. He put the remaining brownie back on the table. He went back to his truck to unload the rest of his things. Sarah walked into the front room and awaited Max to come into the house. She went into the kitchen to prepare plates for dinner. When Max came into the house, Sarah ran over to give him a big hug and a kiss.

"Where are the girls? It's so quiet in here? I wasn't expecting to see that."

"There in their beds sleeping. I told them if they took a nap, time would go by much faster, and you would be home when they woke up."

"So are you thinking what I'm thinking?" Max smiled. Sarah grabbed him by the hand and went outside.

They came back into the house to freshen up for dinner before the girls had any knowledge of them disappearing. The girls were overjoyed when they saw their dad. Lauren called while Max was in the room talking with Hannah and Haven.

"Hey girl, what are you doing?" ask Lauren.

"Nothing really. I'm waiting on Max and the girls to come eat dinner."

"Oh, when did Max get in?"

"About an hour ago."

"Did yall make it rain yet?"

"And you know this, man! The girls were still asleep when he got here."

"I knew yall did. Yawl some freaks."

"Momma did you see Daddy?" asked Haven.

"Yes, honey, I did," Sarah looked at Max and smiled.

"Hey, Max, did you try the brownies?"

"Tell Max I said hey," said Lauren.

"Max, Lauren said hey.

"Tell her I said hey," replied Max. "Hey Lauren, Sarah over here trying to take me out with these hard brownies", Max laughed and smiled at Sarah.

Sarah didn't bother repeating what Max had said about her brownies. Instead, she continued the previous conversation she and Lauren were having. Max sat down on the couch in the front room to eat his dinner while Hannah, Haven, and Sarah sat at the kitchen table. After sitting down to eat, Sarah noticed that Max didn't get the chicken breast to eat; instead, he got the chicken wings.

"Max, why didn't you get the chicken breast. I made it just for you."

Sarah instantly remembered that he doesn't eat his chicken oven fried. *What was I thinking? I totally forgot. He has been gone for so long. I have forgotten how to cook for him. I have become so accustomed to cooking fried chicken in the oven,"* Sarah became worried of Max's response.

"I told you that I don't eat that crap. I don't like trying new food like that." He picked through the food on his plate like a four-year-old who was a picky eater.

Sarah took a deep breath and exhaled. She mumbled, "Boy if I didn't miss him." Sarah became so upset and disgusted with his attitude that she couldn't even enjoy her food, so she got up from the table and threw it away when the girls wasn't looking. She proceeded to wash dishes.

"Hey, Lauren I will call you back when I'm done washing dishes." Said Sarah. She needed time to allow her feelings to dissolve.

"Naw girl gone head and enjoy your man. I'll call you tomorrow.

Sarah continued to wash the dish as she talked to herself saying, *"That's just like Max to say something to hurt my feelings."*

She looked over a Max. *"I keep telling him not to do that, but he says he doesn't know that he's doing anything wrong, and I'm too sensitive."*

Sarah rinse the dishes before drying them with a towel.

"I would never make him feel the way he makes me feel a lot of times, even though I could."

"Thanks for the food babe," Max said as he approached Sarah from behind. He kissed her cheek. He placed his empty plate in Sarah's hand.

"You're welcome." Sarah was still feeling hurt. All she could think about was the fact that she put a lot of thought and effort into making her husband a nice dinner with brownies as a snack, and he was so critical.

Sarah's eyes teared up. One would think that after all these years. He would know when I'm upset. Sarah took a deep breath, but didn't release it right away.

"Man, I can't wait to get this week over with," said Max. "How about you babe?" Max stared at Sarah, awaiting her response.

Sarah nodded her head yes. She walked throughout the kitchen picking up dishes from off the table. Max stared at Sarah from the other room. He was trying to figure out the reason for Sarah's silence.

"You okay?" Max asked in a concerned tone. He leaned forward in his seat.

"I'm okay," She tilted her head to the side in hopes to prevent her tears from falling onto her face were Max could see them.

"Are you sure?"

Sarah nodded her head yes and continued to wash the dishes.

She took a second to evaluate what just happen. She had a brief heart to heart talk with herself. *You walk around here like everything is peaches and cream. Well, I want to tell you it's not.* She sighed. *I have got to get a handle on our relationship, or he's going to continue to treat me according to how he's feeling. If he's happy, we're good, but if he's mad, everything I do gets on his nerves. That makes me so uptight. I can't be myself around him. I can't take this anymore.* She slammed a glass cup on the kitchen table breaking it.

Max jumped up as he was startled by the breaking of the glass.

The girls ran into the kitchen, "Momma what happen? Are you alright?" asked Hannah.

"Nothing, baby. I'm fine. Thanks for asking. Go back to bed."

"Ok, Mommy. I love you, and I love you too, Daddy," said Hannah. She turned and went back to her room, pulling Haven behind her.

"Baby, what's wrong?" Max kept his distance until he figured out the cause of Sarah's behavior.

"What do you think is wrong with me?" she said trying to keep her voice to a minimum. She didn't want to alarm the girls.

"Baby, I don't know. That's why I'm asking." Max seemed very nervous as his voice quivered as he spoke to Sarah.

It was obvious Max had no clue about how she was feeling. She couldn't explain her feelings nor her behavior; this wasn't like Sarah. She would never put herself in danger. Surely she didn't want the girls to see her act this way.

Max stood awaiting answers as Sarah stood debating what to do next. She knew it was too late to play the silent game, since she had already broken the glass. She decided she might as well tell Max how miserable he has made her since they moved.

Sarah broke the silence that has entrapped her for some time now.

Sarah closed her eyes then opened them. She shook her head in disbelief and said, "You were gone for months. You come back and complain like you have the right to. I bust my butt cooking and cleaning for you. Why in God's name did I do that? Not so you can criticize my cooking!" Sarah threw the dish towel in the sink.

"There's the problem right there! Instead of trying to please man, I should have done it because I know it's pleasing to God. That's what the heck I get. You can't please man; they always leave you disappointed. I don't even think you know what you like to eat. You haven't had my cooking in the longest time, yet you toot your nose up? Boy I tell you the truth!" Sarah continued in a snarky tone. "You give a ninja some money, and he begins to think that he's too good for you. Oh, I'm sorry," she said sarcastically, "You always been like that I'm now just get a full dose of it." Sarah picked up the broken glass from off the table.

"Baby where is all this coming from? I'm sorry about talking about the food. I've had a long day. I do appreciate your cooking. Look at me when I'm talking to you," Max said gently and pulled Sarah close to him.

"I don't like what this long distance thing is doing to me. I didn't sign up for this," Sarah started to cry. It's hard not having you here. No, I take that back. With God's strength, I'm able to maintain, but I need you here. I want you here."

"I'm so sorry, baby. I'm here now," Max kissed Sarah on the forehead. Sarah wiped her runny nose and tears on his shirt.

"Baby, come on now; this is one of my favorite shirts." Max laughed in hopes to cheer Sarah up.

No matter how Max made her feel she couldn't hold his actions against him for very long if at all. Later that night Sarah woke up in unbearable pain. She balled up in the bed and screamed.

"Oh my God, it hurts, it hurts Lord, Jesus make it stop," Sarah yelled.

Max jumped up out of his sleep to comfort her. "Are you ok? What can I do? Do you need to go to the hospital?"

"No, just bring me some pain medicine, please," she requested.

Max ran to the bathroom to get two Tylenol tablets.

Sarah filled her mouth with water and tossed the tablets in her mouth and swallowed. She balled up in the bed underneath the covers with a heating pad on her stomach.

Max held Sarah. "Baby if you are not feeling better tomorrow, I'm going to take you to the hospital."

"Okay." Sarah nodded her head.

The next morning Sarah decided she wanted Max to take her to the doctor. They dropped the kids off at Max sister's house before heading to the doctor's office. Max kissed and then rubbed Sarah's stomach as they sat in the doctor's office.

"Baby doll, I think I know what's wrong with you," Max kissed Sarah stomach once more.

"What?" He always had an answer or solution to something.

"I think you are pregnant. Yep, I bet you are. It all makes sense now. You're not on any birth control, you done went all Jackie Chan on me because you're moody, and I have been feelng sick also."

"I don't know. I can't concentrate right now." She grabbed her head as it began to throb.

When they got to the doctor's office, the nurse got them in the examination room rather quickly, and had Sarah do a urine sample. Sarah and Max waited in silence. Sarah's head still throbbed in pain.

Knock, knock. "May I come in?" asked a voice from the other side of the door.

"Yes," Sarah replied.

"Hey doc," said Max as the doctor entered the room.

"I viewed your test results and I want to be the first to say congratulations! You're pregnant."

Sarah gasped. "How far along?"

"You're eight weeks. I wrote you a prescription for vitamins and iron pills. You may continue to experience pain; if so, you can take Tylenol only. Any other pain medication could harm the baby."

Sarah sat in shock as she thought back on Pastor Edwards and Pastor Smith mentioning a baby as it pertained to her.

"Ok, thanks, Doctor. "Max smiled. "Ay Doc, I told her she was pregnant, but she didn't want to believe me."

While riding to pick up their girls, Sarah text all her friends and family.

"I have been so moody and sick lately. I have lost and gained weight. Max and I just found out that we're pregnant. I stand corrected: I'm pregnant."

Max and Sarah received several text messages saying, "Congratulations on the new baby."

They changed their minds about picking the girls up after receiving a text from his sister.

"Hey, Sarah go home and get some rest. I'll drop the girls

off later."

When they arrived back, home Max ran Sarah a much-needed hot bath. He lit scented candles around the bathroom. She soaked in the tub for about two hours before getting out. She slipped into her robe and walked into the bed where she heard soft, soothing music.

"Hey baby doll come here," Max said.

Sarah walked over to Max and stood in front of him. He kissed her belly. Sarah lay down on her back and closed her eyes. Max reached for the baby oil gel. He poured a generous amount onto his hand.

"Ah, that feels so good. I can't put in words how much I miss you, Max." Sarah smiled feeling relaxed.

"Well, you can get use to me being around. I can't leave you here by yourself you're carrying my baby. I don't want you to be stressed out or anything."

She smiled slightly. She knew that it was only a matter of time before what he said was just something he said with no meaning behind it.

Max proceeded to give Sarah a full body massage until she was completely relaxed and submitted to sleep.

Six and a half months into Sarah's pregnancy, after several weeks of trying to find the perfect name for their bundle of joy, Sarah and Max decided that they would name their baby after Sarah's favorite cousin if it's a girl and Max's nephew if it's a boy. Today was an exciting day for Max and Sarah. Sarah got dressed and gathered everything she needed for her doctor's appointment. She was anticipating the results; however, she hated she had to find out alone. Sarah arrived at her doctor's appointment as scheduled. She was put in her room and told to lay down on the table and relax. The doctor raised her shirt and applied a cold gel to her stomach. The doctor placed the monitor on her belly and allowed Sarah to listen to its heart beat. Sarah smiled as she listen and watched the monitor as her active baby moved about.

"What are you wanting the sex to be?" The doctor asked Sarah.

"A boy. However, my husband wants another girl. He likes the idea of having mini me's running around." Sarah chuckled. "Oddly the ones we have don't look like me."

"Do you want to know what you're having?" The doctor smiled looking up at Sarah.

"Yes, but not right now."

"Are you going to do a big reveal?"

"Not really. Max started a new job about two months ago here in Mississippi. Unfortunately, his new job didn't allow him to take off today, so I want us to find out together."

"Sounds great. I'll have the nurse put the ultrasound in an envelope indicating what you're having."

"Thank you."

The nurse brought Sarah the envelope and a appointment card with her next appointment on it. Sarah stopped to get a slushy from Sonic's hamburger restaurant before going home. She got a call from Max.

"Hey baby doll. How did your doctor's visit go?"

"It went great."

"So, what are we having?"

"I don't know. I told the doctor to put the ultrasound in an envelope. I want both of us to find out at the same time."

"Ok baby doll, sounds good. How's baby Aliya doing was she moving a lot during your doctor's visit."

"Baby *Alex* is doing fine. He was moving more than usual during my visit."

They both laughed.

"I bet it's a girl."

"We will see wont we. I just made it home. I'm going to get a nap in before the girls arrive home from school."

"Ok baby I'll see you when I come home from work."

Sarah smiled. "The words come home from work sound so good together."

They both laughed before hanging up the phone.

When the girls made it home Sarah went to the print shop and got print on two onesies. She had a pink onesies that said

Baby Aliya and a blue that said Baby Alex. She then went to a party store and had the onesies placed inside two separate balloons, a pink one for Aliya and a blue one for Alex. Once they made it home, they all at dinner and bath before the big reveal. Sarah instructed Hannah to read the word on the ultrasound, and whichever one says boy or girl, she is to have Haven pop the balloon that goes with the ultrasound. Sarah and Max sat on the couch waiting on Hannah to open the envelope.

Hannah smiled as she pulled out the ultrasound. She read it then bent down and whispered into Havens ear.

Haven laughed. She took the pin and popped the pink balloon.

"I knew it!" Max yelled.

Haven popped the other balloon.

"Wait what?" Sarah heart pounded harder. She stood up. "There's two."

Max looked at Sarah's stomach. "That can't be right."

Sarah took the ultrasound out of Hannah's hand.

She closed her eyes and took a deep breath as she stared at the ultrasound. "I can't believe this. Oh my God. What are we going to do?" Sarah sat down. She looked sad.

"What's wrong baby?" Max was concerned. "Let me see." He reached over to grab the ultrasound.

Sarah stood up turning her back towards Max. "I can't let you see this. You're not going to like it."

"Like what? Baby, stop playing." Max tried reaching around Sarah to get the ultrasound.

"Bam! It's a boy. Now didn't I tell you that?"

They rejoiced with laughter, and they all went to bed.

Sarah was enjoying Max being home. They have been working on reestablishing their love for one another. Max had reconnected with the kids. He got a job that was an hour and a half from their house in Mississippi. He was coming home every day. Sarah was sure he liked his new job; he didn't say anything negative about it —well at least she didn't allow him to complain to her about his job. The job was expected to last a year if not longer, and it seemed promising to Sarah. Max came home from work smiling. He walked into the kitchen where she stood washing dishes. He kissed her on the cheek before looking into the pantry for a snack.

"Hey, baby doll."

"Hey, how's it going?"

"Well, baby, I quit my job," Max grinned.

"Really, What? What happen? Why would you do that?" Sarah asked Max. *Dang it. Here we go,* Sarah thought to herself.

"The boss made me mad, so I got my stuff and left the job," Max said so proudly.

"Oh." Sarah was dumbfounded.

Sarah figured normally quitting a job would be something a husband would talk over with his wife before he did it to insure the family had enough money saved up. *Not my Max. Mr. I'm Max-Houston-I-can-get-another-job.* Wow. Sarah shook her head. *Only my husband,* she thought to herself.

"I'll call the hall in the morning and see what jobs they have available." Max gazed into Sarah's eyes.

"Well have you thought about starting your own company? You know, like we talked about?"

"No, I'm not ready yet."

"What are you waiting on? You have been doing this for how many years now? Twelve?"

"I've been doing this for fourteen years."

"You have a ton of friends. They always call you looking for work. You have gotten people hired on different jobs. You come highly recommended whenever a new project starts. You have been to several states to work, and many companies know you. Babe, you can start a company and make millions, not the thousands you're making that now. I'm talking about eight figures, and that's after taxes. Baby, we need to dream big, think outside the box. I don't want to be average. With the money you earn, we should be balling, but we're not; we're still in debt somehow. We are living pay check to pay check. You have made more money in a week than some people make in a month."

Max stared at Sarah in silence as he reminisced about the things he used to do before they moved to Mississippi.

"Hello Max! Back to Earth, Max!" Sarah yelled. He sat at the kitchen table in a daze.

"Huh?"

"I said, what are you afraid of when it comes to starting your own business? I can do all the proper paperwork. Did you forget I was an office manager for a construction company for seven years? I can see it now: 'Houston's Welding Company,'" Sarah smiled. "A man without vision will perish."

"I know baby, I have a vision, but I just don't have the money right now to pursue it," Max sighed.

Max searched for a job in Mississippi every day. The aftermath of him quitting his previous job put them in a financial bind. He was blackballed. He was not allowed to work on jobs down south for sixty days because he quit. Their bills came rolling in on schedule, and they were still a month behind on all of them. Max had to go off to work again. To Sarah this felt like an ongoing break up between two confused lovers. Max went to work in Louisiana for three weeks; this job consisted of him working twelve-hour shifts a day sevens straight. When the job ended, Max went to Memphis and worked for three weeks, he was working ten-hour days, seven days a week . Birmingham was the last job Max worked on before he came home. He worked ten-hour shifts, seven days for two weeks.

Before Max could make it home and relax, the calls from his friends came rolling in. They informed him of different states that had work. Max's BA (Business Agent) called him to see if he was working. A BA is assigned to an Ironworker, and ensures that the Ironworker stays employed. The BA gets paid as long as the Ironworker is working. Max's BA informed him that they had a job opening in Starkville, Mississippi building a power plant. The manager over the job requested that Max be assigned to this job if possible. They needed him to be at work in the morning if he wasn't working.

Max informed his BA that he had just left a job in

Birmingham, and he needed a couple of days to rest. His BA told him to rest; he will let the job know he will be able to start work Saturday.

Max started working on the job in Starkville three days later. However, the girls and Sarah became invisible. The job required him to work 14-hour shifts. Sarah and Max never spent time with each other. It was like he wasn't even there. Hannah and Haven never got to see their dad because they were already sleeping when Max got home from work. One day, when Max came home, Sarah voiced her concern about him not making time for her and their girls.

"Max can I talk to you for a second?"

"Sure," Max sat down beside Sarah on the couch.

"The girls and I miss you. We never get to spend time with you anymore. We haven't been to the movies or out to eat in a very long time. I can't remember the last time we had sex."

"Babe, really, that's how you feel? We just had sex the other day. You forgot?"

"Oh, we did, didn't we? I don't know. I'm having mixed emotions. I don't know if it's the baby or what. The kids barely see you; it's like I'm a single parent with great benefits. I need you to start making time for us. The girls need you in their life-- not just financially, but physically, mentally, emotionally, and most important spiritually. You are the head of this family. Little girls need to have a relationship with their dad. I wouldn't have it any other way. You know I'm a daddy's girl, and having my dad in my life help mold me to be the woman I am today. You remind me so much of my dad. He was a great provider; however, he knew how to separate work and home.

For a quick second, Sarah thought maybe she was asking too much of Max. The conversation between Max and Sarah didn't go over well. For some strange reason, Max felt like Sarah was calling him a terrible husband and a no-good father. He gave Sarah the silent treatment for days, but by the time he decided to speak to her, she had determined that they needed some time apart, so she wrote him a letter expressing her feelings. She arranged for her siblings to come get her and the girls from Mississippi. Her siblings preferred she didn't drive because she was seven months pregnant, depressed, and lonely. They said she was high risk for suicide, and they didn't want her to be alone.

Sarah's family reunion, the one Max never attended, was scheduled around the time Sarah planned to leave Max. A perfect getaway Sarah knew Max wouldn't suspect any foul play, and that's how she wanted it. Before Max read the letter, she wanted to be long gone. She didn't want to fall victim to his ability to woo her into staying with him. Sarah left the letter in their bedroom in the center of the bed. Her siblings had arrived at their house in Mississippi right before Max left for work. They packed Sarah and the girls' bags in the truck. The girls were still sleepy when Max put them into the truck.

"I love you; I'm going to miss you all," Max kissed Sarah on the lips before kissing her belly.

"I love you too," Sarah smiled slightly giving Max a long hug, one that he would soon cherish if she decided not to return to him.

When Sarah looked in the rearview mirror, her visual of Max became smaller as the agonizing pain in her chest grew larger.

Hannah, Haven and Sarah's brother Jimmy was in the back seat sleep. Sarah sat in the front seat with her other brother James, who was driving.

"So, did you tell the kids?" James asked.

"No. I didn't have the courage to tell them we may not be coming back, so I decided not to tell them. Was that wrong?" Sarah felt a little convicted.

"No. It might be better that way for now."

"I feel bad though. When I was leaving, it was like Max knew."

"What do you mean? Did you tell him anything?"

"No."

"Were you acting different?"

"No."

"Well, why do you think he knows?"

"I don't know he had this sad look on his face. I've never seen him look like that before. I'll never forget it; it was like he was heartbroken."

"You're over thinking it. You are going out of town. What man wouldn't be sad to see his wife leave without him?"

"I just wish I could have held him a little while longer."

"Man, here we go. You know it's never too late to change your mind. After all, it was your idea. You said you wanted him to do better. Now here's your chance to let him. Now get it together. You have a plan, and you need to follow through with it."

"I'm good. I'm going to go through with it," Sarah said with confidence.

"Are you sure?"

"Yes."

"Have you considered the affect this will have on the kids?"

"Yes-- I mean, no. I'm taking it one day at a time. I got this, trust me. To be honest, I don't even think me leaving Max would affect them at all in their eyes; he's already gone because they hardly get to see him." Sarah stared out the window.

"Ok, I just want to make sure you're doing what's best for you and the kids. You will be introducing them to the world that's not so familiar, and I'm afraid this may have a huge impact on their lives. I know you say it seems like he's already gone, but he's still there physically, so it's not the same." James glanced at Sarah.

Sarah turned toward James. "Look, I know what I'm doing! quit asking me if I'm sure; you're making me have second thoughts about the situation, and that's not what I want, so stop asking." Sarah became upset. "I know my options, and I'm going through with it. This is the only way. I will know if I made the right decision soon enough. They say if you love something let it go, and if it comes back to you, then you know it was meant to be."

"Hum, I'm not sure you can use that with your situation," he laughed.

Sarah felt a sharp pain in her stomach, it felt as if she were having contractions. *Not this early,* Sarah thought. Maybe it was from sitting too long and crossing over the bridge in Memphis going into Arkansas. It was kind of bumpy.

She leaned back in her seat trying to relax, in hopes to calm baby Alex down. He was kicking her butt, pushing his hands and feet up against her stomach as if he was trying to break free. While in the process of putting her mind and body in a peaceful state, Sarah felt a tap on her shoulder; the spontaneous touch made her jump hard and break into an instant sweat.

"Are you ready to do this?" Nathen asked.

"Yes, I already sent Max a text telling him that my phone has been acting crazy, and I may not be able to answer when he calls."

"And he was ok with that."

"Yes, he trusts me. I'm his wife remember."

"Uh, if you say so. If my wife ever tried to pull some mess like you doing, I think I would honestly hurt her no bull…. You know it's never too late to change your mind."

"I know, Nathan! Quit trying to change my mind!

"I know, man, it's just, you are my lil sister. I don't want you to mess up and lose a good dude, all because you think you can do better, or you need your space, or whatever the case maybe. I told you when you became serious that the grass is not always greener on the other side. You may feel like your grass is dying but sometimes all it needs is a little TLC to get it back to what it used to be. I love you. I'm not going to tell you anything wrong. In the end, all I can do is tell you. Sometimes I think you too dang smart for your own good. I'm not sure what you're trying to accomplish by doing this, but whatever it is, I hope it works out for you," Nathan said, digressing from the conversation. He looked as if he was very disappointed in Sarah.

About eight hours later Sarah, her girls, and two brothers arrived at their mom's house. James and Nathan worked together putting Sarah and the girls luggage into the house.

Sarah got out of the truck and opened the back door to reach inside to get Haven. Her stomach began to cramp.

"Hey, James," Sarah yelled, "can you take Haven in the house for me? My stomach is hurting."

"Alright," James grabbed Haven from out of the truck.

"Hey, what's going on?" Sarah's mom yelled out the door as she stood in the doorway waiting for Sarah to come into the house.

"Nothing, my stomach's cramping."

"Are you sure that you're not having baby Alex? That was a long drive."

"I don't think so, I'm only seven in a half months."

"Well, I'll be in the house if you need me." She walked back into the house.

"Ok."

"So now that you're here, what's the plan? Did you tell my momma?" asked Nathan.

"No. However, she did agree to keep the girls this summer."

"What! How did that happen? Let me guess: you bribed her with money and contraband."

Sarah laughed "No. Now you know you can't bribe your momma. If she doesn't want to do something then she is not going to do it."

"Yeah, you right. She never agrees to watch my kids. I just drop them off and leave," Nathan laughed.

"Yeah. Now she never wants to watch anyone else's kids because you do that so much. I was shocked when she said she would watch them. I just knew she would say no. I guess she misses them." Sarah held her stomach after Alex kicked her with full force.

"You ok."

"I'm not sure. I hope so."

"Ay girl, now you know you too dang old to be peeing on yourself. Ay Momma, I think you need to potty train your daughter again because she out here pissing-- I mean peeing on herself," Nathan laughed uncontrollably. "Where is my phone?

I have to record this." Nathan searched his pockets for his phone.

"I'm not peeing on myself, stupid, my water just broke," Sarah spoke calmly.

Sarah never experienced her water breaking on its on. She had scheduled C-sections with both Hannah and Haven.

"Momma! Sarah's water just broke, bring your operating kit, stat. Hurry up so you can deliver this baby."

"What? Shut up, fool! She is not about to operate on me. Call an ambulance."

"Girl, you are tripping! My momma can deliver your baby with her eyes closed. Do I need to remind you of how many dogs and cats she helps deliver?" Nathan took a long pause, then laughed.

"Nathan!" Sarah yelled. "Don't you have a phone in your hand?

"Yeah, why?" he looked confused and frantic.

"Call an ambulance, duh."

"What do I say? My sister about to have her third litter?"

Sarah's mom yelled as she stood on the front porch. "I told her butt he was going to come, but she didn't want to listen to me. I called the ambulance they should be on their way."

"Alex says you not about to do his daddy like that, he coming out to put a stop to this mess," Nathan laughed as he took pictures of Sarah's facial expressions.

"Shut up, Nathan, you stupid!"

Sarah couldn't help but laugh at him as he walked her into the house. However, the laughter didn't stop the contractions from abusing her physically and taking a mental toll on her.

"Do you want me to call the baby's daddy?" asked James.

"No, no, don't let anybody call and tell him anything. If you do, I will jack you up and never talk to you again."

"What? Girl, you are tripping. You don't want him to know? you not right."

"Shut up! I can't think right now, stop talking to me. Ah, I can't take it. I need drugs. Give me drugs. Please."

"Dang, Sarah why would you wait until you became

pregnant to become a geek-err," James shook his head.

The ambulance pulled up in no time, and EMTs came into the house with a stretcher to put Sarah on.

"This will be over soon," Sarah's mom assured her. Before the paramedic put Sarah in the ambulance, she kissed Sarah on the forehead.

I can honestly say my mom becomes extra motherly whenever I have kids. That's the one time we actual get along. Sarah thought to herself.

James and Nathan followed behind the ambulance. Sarah arrived at the hospital ten minutes later. They rushed her into an emergency room. They gave her some meds to sooth the pain while they ran some test. Sarah's mom siblings and children sat in the ER waiting room. After an hour the doctor came out to get Sarah's mother and sister to go back to Sarah's room to visit here while Nathan and James stayed with the girls.

"Knock, Knock." Said Sarah's mom pushing the curtain open and walking into Sarah's room.

Sarah looked up at her mom and Evans and shook her head.

"What's all that for?" asked Evan's.

Sarah mom rubbed Sarah's stomach. "How's my grand baby?"

"He's fine."

"Why are you still pregnant? I thought your water broke?"

"Me too. False alarm." Sarah sadden her face.

"So if that wasn't your water breaking then what was it." Evans disfigured her face.

Sarah laughed. "Nathan was right. I peed on myself."

They all laughed.

"But you said you were cramping." Said Evans.

"Yeah those cramps or normal. A pregnant woman with a weak bladder who has the tendency to overreact equals false alarm."

The doctor wanted Sarah to stay at least one night in the hospital to get some rest. He saw that her stress levels were high. Sarah's siblings left the hospital and Sarah's mom took the girls home with her.

When night time fell upon Sarah, so did her emotions. She couldn't believe Max wasn't here with her. A part of her felt it was for the best, but her spirit man informed her otherwise.

What if I had baby without Max? He would be crushed and I'm not sure how our relationship would be after it, especially if he knew my intentions maybe to leave him, Sarah pondered.

CHAPTER ELEVEN

Summer had come around in full force. Sarah felt she needed to get away. She arranged for Hannah and Haven to stay with her mother for the summer while she stayed with her Godsister Lisa in Virginia. In hopes to relive a lot of her stress she boarded the plane to Virginia. Lisa picked

"Hey Lisa."

"Hey. Wow you have gotten so big." Lisa rubbed Sarah stomach before giving her a hug. "How are you doing, Sarah?"

"Free," Sarah chuckled.

"I take it you still not talking to Max."

"Nope. I had little to no communication with Max since the last time I saw him. We text one another and that's it. He would ask how the girls and I were doing."

"So, you mean to tell me he still don't know you left him."

Sarah shrugged. "I guess not. I'm not surprised. He gets so caught up in work and forgets to breathe. He's working fourteen hour shifts now seven days a week, so he practically lives at the job. I bet the letter I wrote him is still sitting on the bed. He doesn't sleep in our bed if I'm not there. When he works hours like that, his routine is work, sleep, work, and he may eat a little something every now and then, and bathe every blue moon."

"Shut up, girl. You silly. How you just gon' say that man take baths once every blue moon?" Lisa laughed out loud. "So are you going to change your number?"

"I don't want to cut off contact with him completely; after all, I'm going back home, I just don't know when."

"That makes sense."

Several weeks had passed. According to Sarah, the days at the beach didn't feel the same without her little family. She missed her goofy, lovable girls and her handsome husband.

"Oh, how I love that man." said Sarah. She started to question the decision she made to leave him. "Oh, how I would do anything to hear his voice."

She picked up her phone and dialed Max's cell phone private, in hopes he would answer since he never answers blocked calls. When the phone started to ring, Sarah's nervousness grew and lingered after every ring. She removed the phone from her ear after the third ring so she could hang up the phone. She heard Max say, "Hello" and clear his throat.

Tears ran down Sarah's face as his voice sent chills down her spine. She could hear the loneliness in his voice. She knew by now he was missing her and the girls. Sarah sat holding the phone in silence.

"Well, since you're not going to say anything, I'm going to hang up. You can call me back when you're ready to talk," Max hung up his phone. Sarah sat on the couch looking through pictures of her and Max.

Sarah later called her mother to check on the girls. "They are preoccupied with playing with their cousin." There was a brief silence between the two before Sarah's mother continued on with the conversation. "Sarah, your hubby called to talk to the girls today."

"He did? What did you say to him?" asked Sarah. She

became fearful that her mother had told Max something.

"Nothing. He asked if you were around, and I told him no and that you were with your girlfriends. When are you going home, child? That man is missing you. He is really hurting; you can hear it in his voice."

"I know, he'll be alright, in time, he will heal."
"I don't know, child. You shouldn't do him like that; you putting him at risk of being in a very dark place. Trust me. I know these things. I'm your mother."
"Hmm, you didn't tell him I was in Virginia did you?"
"No, child. I'm about to get off this phone with you. What you are doing is wrong. I'm not going to keep lying for you neither."
"I'll call back later so I can talk to the girls."
"Ok," Sarah's mom replied. "I love you. I hope you taking care of yourself and my grandbaby while you're up there."
Sarah walked outside and sat on the front porch. She received a text from Max.
"Today is July 12, 2012. Three weeks from today at two o'clock p.m. I'm supposed to be taking my wife to the hospital to deliver our baby boy. Instead I'm sitting here so hurt and resentful, looking at a picture of my beautiful wife and kids who I haven't seen and barely heard from you since they left me about two months ago. I just want you to know that I love you. I want you back—no, I need you back, along with the girls. I call my mother-in-law's house every day to talk to the girls. I miss them so much. It's sad they don't even know what's going on. I guess that's a good thing. I'm hurting. I haven't been eating like I should, and now I regret taking your cooking for granted. I'm ready to quit my job, and say forget everything and move out of town. I can't take it being in this house without you. I keep moving, pushing forward, praying asking God to bring you back to me. I'm asking Him to change

me for you, for us, so we can be happy. I won't quit my job because I still have to provide for my family. I've been sending your mother money for the girls. I also send her money for keeping them. I've been putting money into your account. That's for you to keep. You can do whatever you want with it. I want to know how you and baby Alex is doing. Can you send me a picture? However long it takes I'll be here for you. I will continue to love you no matter where you are."

Sarah stood up to take a picture of her while holding her stomach.
Her phone rang.
"What's up sis?" Evans asked. "How are you and the baby doing?"
"We're good."
"Lately, I have been thinking about you and Max. Have you talk to him?"
"Yes-- I mean no. I called him, earlier today but I didn't say anything." Sarah laughed. "I wanted to hear his voice."
"And how many times a day do you do that?"
Sarah Laughed. "Not often enough. He can't have his phone on him at this job, so I'm lucky to catch him. I may not do it anymore because he will think someone is playing on his phone and change his number. He did send me a text telling me how much he missed me and wanted a picture of me and baby Alex ,so I sent him one."

"Awe girl that's so sweet. I feel sorry for him.
"I guess he did find the letter I wrote him."
"So have you thought about when you are going home or coming back to Saint Louis?"
"No. That's if I go back."
"Girl you crazy! Take your butt home! What's wrong with you? How could you not see that this man loves you? What man you know is about to continue to provide for his

wife and her mother after she just up and disappeared on him. No dangone body! I love you sis and I want you to be happy. Max a good dude and it's sad that everybody see it but you. You get on my nerves sometimes acting like a spoil brat."

Sarah rolled her eyes. "Are you done yet? I know he's a great guy."

"Yes, I'm done for now."

"I talked to my momma today. She was upset that I haven't went back home yet.

"Sarah, you never did tell me why you left Max in the first place."

"I just had to get away so I wouldn't cheat." That was one of the reason three reasons.

"Really? Was it that bad? Are you talking about the close encounter you had with the school principal?"

"That's so nasty. I wouldn't have done it tho. I'm not even going to lie: at the time, I was seeking a little attention. I wanted to see if I could get him to take an interest in me. Max wasn't giving me enough attention, if any at all. He was always gone. I promise he acts like not having sex doesn't bother me."

Sarah had been dealing with some issues before she married Max, but she was to afraid to tell him about her slight addiction.

"My flesh wanted to find out if I still had it going on, but in all honesty, I shouldn't have been turning tricks on the devil's playground. He doesn't play fair."

"So be honest. Do you think you would've pursued an affair with the principal? If it was just you and him in his office? After school and all the teachers and students were gone? Let's say it's been a month since you saw Max."

"Heck no! Max has been away from home longer than that once before. I had no problem keeping my cat in the bag."

"Ok, well let's just say you are extremely hungry you haven't been with Max in three months. The principal looks delicious in gray slacks with a black button up shirt with his tie loosened after a long day of work with two more hours to go. He looks restless, yet sexy as heck. He got on that cologne you love so much; you know which one I'm talking about-- that Chrome Azzaro's Live to inspire. You went out and bought Max the same kind because it smelled so good. You said it sent you sailing every time you smelled it. You had to restrain yourself with chains to keep you away."

"That's just like the devil to paint a pretty picture for you."

"So would you," she waited silently for Sarah's answer.

"Hmm," Sarah mumbled. She thought back to that day in the principal office. She never mention this day to Evans.

"I stood over him and waited until he got up out of his seat. We switched spots, and he pushed the chair in for me. "How nice of you to do that. Thank you," I said smiling. "So what do you want me to type?"

"You can type as I talk. Can you handle that?"

"Sure, I can handle anything you can spit out." I said jokingly.

"Watch it now, Mrs. Houston. That sounds like a challenge to me. I love to compete." He stood behind her grinning.

Sarah turned her head and looked at him, as if she was going to challenge him.

"Oh, I'm sorry. Am I too close? I can move."

"No, you're fine," She smirked and took a deep overdue swallow.

"Ok, 29, 34, 55, 235," as he talked, my hearing became impaired. He reached over me with his left hand and grabbed his phone from off his desk as it rang. A soft, pleasant breeze of Live to Inspire cologne brushed my nose, followed by a shock wave of intimate emotions that plunged throughout my body. I indulged heavily as my physical physique took a rocky trip of corrupt pleasure.

"Hello." Evans screamed through the phone interrupting Sarah's moment.

Sarah cleared her throat. "Evans, please shut up. I will never cheat on my husband. I love God too much to break His covenant. Stop planting seductive and unpleasant adulterous spirits in my life. I don't want them."

"It took you long enough to answer. You must had a flash back or something."

"Well, I was trying to see how far you were going to take this nonsense, but that was my fault; I should have stopped you a long time ago."

Evans scoffed. "That sounds so crazy to me. Please help me to understand: you won't cheat on your husband because of the covenant you made with God. However, you just left your husband, for whatever reason you care not to share with me? I don't think God would approve of what you're doing. I know the Bible doesn't say anything about being temporarily separated from your spouse while you get yourself together. Your vows said for better or worse, sickness and in health. You're leaving that door open to cheat or to be cheated on. Remember that you are still human, and from what I know, your flesh is a beast trying to win the battle over your spirit man. Surely you didn't consult Godly counsel on this."

Sarah sat in silence, quoting scriptures in her head: *"without advice plans go wrong, but with many advisers they succeed.*

Where no counsel is, the people fall: but in the multitude of counselors there is safety. For the proper time and procedure for every matter, though a person may be weighed down by misery."

Sarah knew Evans was right, but she wasn't trying to face the truth about her situation right now. "I have to let my phone charge. I'll talk to you later."

"Ok. Mary." Evans said unplayfully referring to Jesus' mother Mary in the Bible.

Sarah hung up the phone feeling like her spirit man had been tampered with. She knew when she decided to leave her husband that she was going to be out of the will of God; nonetheless, she felt she just had to do her for a while, at least until she got herself together.

CHAPTER TWELVE

After a long day of work, back Max came home. He inserted the key into the front door and turned it. He pushed the door open widely and stood in the doorway. He sighed looking at the dusty family portraits that Sarah sometimes dusted that hung on the wall in the front room. Max went into Hannah and Haven's room and looked around as he stood in the doorway. He noticed the girls left their clothes all over their bedroom floor when they left for Saint Louis. He realized that he had not been in the girl's room since they left. He picked up their clothes from off the floor and put them in a pile on the bed and began to fold them. He reminisced on the times they spent together followed by missed birthdays, parent teacher's conference, family reunions, and Donuts with Dad Day at school. He felt as if he neglected his kids-- not financially but physically, emotionally and possibly mentally.

Sarah did the right thing leaving me, Max thought to himself. *I was never here for them. How could I be so stupid?* Max lay back in Haven's bed and prayed until he fell asleep.

Feeling nervous, Sarah called Max but didn't get an answer, so she walked into the restaurant and sat down at the table. The table had three large jars filled with colored water and floating candles of her favorite colors: pink, yellow, and white. A beautiful pattern of white, pink, and yellow rose petals surrounded the table. Sarah's phone rang.

"Hello?" Sarah answered in a shy tone.

"Hey, I saw that you called me. Is everything ok?" Max asked. He was looking at Sarah in a camera he had placed inside a candle on the table she was sitting at.

"Uh, yeah I was calling because the kids wanted to talk to you before they went to bed."

"Oh, how are you doing?"

"I'm ok, I'm sitting at this restaurant waiting on Lauren. Lately, someone has been sending me flowers. That's just weird."

Sarah didn't think for a second that Max had been sending her those flowers because he hadn't done it in a very long time. "This is a very nice place-- a little too romantic for two women to be having dinner there."

"Hey, I have to get going. They're calling me back to work. I hope you enjoy yourself."

"Hey, Max." Sarah hesitated.

"Yeah, I'm here," Max smiled.

"I really miss you. I would do anything to see you right now." A tear rolled down Sarah's face. "This is a charming place. Maybe we could come here one day," Sarah pressed her lips together as she awaited Max's response.

"Yeah, that would be nice. Be careful out there. Depending on my work schedule we might be able to visit that restaurant sooner than you think. How does that sound?" Sarah smiled as she danced in her seat. "That sounds great; you have not because you ask not, right?"

"Right. that is the Word. Sarah? Were you just dancing?" Max laughed as he observed her from the camera.

"Of course not! Why would I be doing that?" Sarah laughed and began to blush. "I'll let you get back to work. I'll have the girls call you in the morning."

Sarah hung up the phone and continued to wait on Lauren. Lauren arrived at the restaurant late as usual.

"Girl, it's ten minutes after! Where have you been?" Sarah demanded.

"Girl, chill out. I had to set something up," Lauren explained. After they had eaten dinner, they talked for a while then prepared to leave the restaurant.

"Hey, Sarah, check out my new shoes. I bought them for myself yesterday." Lauren pulled out her phone to show Sarah the picture she took of her new shoes.

"Those are cute. Why didn't you buy me a pair? Just selfish." Sarah said jokingly.

"Who said I didn't?"

"Ugh, I don't have them in my possession."

"They are in my car. I will give them to you when we leave."

"Hey, Mrs. Houston."

Sarah jumped and tried to turn around. She had been longing for this moment since she left home without even knowing it, and now it was here--Max's voice in her ear.

"Don't move," said Max while standing behind her. Sarah could feel her body preparing to launch. The warm touch from his hand was all too familiar. The sound of his voice made her melt internally.

Sarah looked at Lauren and whispered, "Is that Max?" She developed excitement while her body performed CPR on her heart because it had stopped.

Sarah smiled. "Yes. Have fun, girl." She got up from the table to leave.

"I'm going to blindfold you now. I want you to take my hand and follow me. Don't worry. I'm not going to hurt you." Sarah got up from the table with a blindfold on and did exactly what Max instructed her to do, closing the door behind them.

Bang, Bang, Bang! There were several loud knocks on the door. Max jumped up out of his pleasure filled sleep and ran to the door. He looked out the front window. He opened the door.

"What's up man? What's going on?" asked Max.

"You tell me," replied Derrick. I have been trying to call you for like a month now. That's not like us to not talk to each other. Is everything okay?"

"Yeah, I'm good," Max answered groggily. "I've been working long hours. You know how it is."

"Yeah, you sure you weren't in a coma? Everyone I talk to said that they haven't heard from you."

Max chuckled.

"I stop by to check on you and to run this business idea by you. Man clean yourself up, I want to treat you to lunch."

Derrick evaluated Max's wellbeing. "Ay man you need some crackers or something? You are skinny as heck!" Derrick opened the front door to leave out.

"Do you think she's coming back? Sarah?" Max asked in hopes to get a good answer. "It's been two months. I really miss her. I don't know what to do. It feels like I'm dying every day, and I don't know how to stop it. I thought about stopping the pain, but that would mean I would have to stop thinking about her, and I don't want to do that. My faith is shaky right now. I'm still trying to hold on. I think that she's coming back. I believe that she's going to walk through the door with my kids, drop her bags in the middle of the floor and say, 'honey I'm home.' I haven't spoken to her our only means of communication is texting. I would do anything to just hear her voice right now. She has a soft, sweet, sexy voice that make my…..

"Max! TMI!" Derrick cut Max off. He looked uncomfortable.

"I'm just saying. But I do talk to the kids almost every day. That's something I haven't done in a long time. It felt right to do that. She hasn't cut me off completely, so I have to ask again: do you think she's coming back? What would you do if your wife Mattie ever left you?"
Derrick cleared his throat. "Well, what you don't know is," Derrick hesitated. "before Mattie, I was married to another woman."
Max raised his head. He looked at Derrick in shock.

"Yeah, we were married for two years, and she said she couldn't do the long distance thing. A lot of people don't know that because that's a part of my past that I have barricaded. We had premarital sex and the girl became pregnant. So to cover up our sin, we married without God's consent. I didn't want anyone to judge me and cast me out the church based on my actions. Truth be told, some church people can be so judgmental and cruel. My ex-wife talked bad to me and treated me as if I was dirt. She would call me everything but a child of God. She told me she was going to cheat on me, and she did. I felt as if the way she was treating me was God's way of punishing me for disobeying him by marrying her.

"We tried to work out our problems after she committed adultery. I forgave her, but every time I thought about that other man laying with her, I became angry and hated her for what she did to our family even more. We separated and got back together. We were happy one minute, then the next, we were at each other's throats. Come to find out, the guy she cheated on me for cheated on her, and she tried getting back at him by getting back with me. We found out she was pregnant, but she didn't know who the daddy was, so I got a divorce to prevent myself from putting my hands on her and possibly hurting her. The wounds she left where like pits of hell, and I thought I would never heal after our divorce was finalized.

"But from there, my walk with God became stronger. He healed me and mended my broken heart. She put me through hell, often times I had to pinch myself to make sure I was still on earth. She was difficult. Nothing I did was good enough. She left me broke-- not just financially, but mentally, physically, and spiritually. I didn't know what to do. I didn't know who to turn to but God. I called on Him before, but this time I meant it. I needed Him. He knew it, and therefore He was right there for me. He said, "I will never leave you, nor forsake you," and I believed him. I don't really know what's going on within your relationship. There's always two sides to a story. Make sure you're doing everything you're supposed to be doing as her husband, and most importantly as a man of God.

"You have to pray and ask God if there's anything you could be doing to better the situation. Even though I knew I gave my ex-wife everything she could ever want, I also failed to realize how much I neglected being there for her physically and mentally when she needed me the most. I thought being a good provider was the major part in a marriage, but I was wrong. As God began to mold me in His image, He showed me where I messed up in my marriage. Turns out that all the things my ex-wife did to me was a chain reaction from me not being there for her. From that, I learned how to treat Mattie. I don't know Sarah's side or how she feels and neither do you. We assume it's something else, but it could be something entirely different. It may not even be you. It may be something she is dealing with. Since you can't talk to her, you need to talk to God about it. Dude, why am I even telling you this? You know God. I know you know Him. You need to reconnect with Him like never before. Continue to have faith and believe, if Sarah is whom you want. Seek His kingdom. You know the rest. Let us pray."

Max stood up, wiping tears from his eyes, and bowed his head.

"Heavenly Father," Derrick started. "I ask that you be with my friend, Max, in his time of need. Lord, I ask that you give him the answers that he's seeking. If it is your will Lord, bring Sarah back to him, mend their marriage, and fill in the gaps. Oh, Lord I come up against the spirit of hatred, jealousy, and adultery and unforgiveness. Satan, you have got to go! Take your hand off their marriage! Bless their children, Lord. When you bring her back, Lord, let him not forget the things that you have taught him. Have him to slow down and appreciate his wife and children that you have blessed him with. We will never fail to give you the honor, the praise, and the glory in Jesus name, Amen."

"Amen." Max said. "Man, I thank you for coming to check on me. I just needed some time to myself. Give me an hour, and I can meet you at the restaurant for lunch, where are we meeting again?" Max asked, looking confused.

"Mamma Know Best in Meridian, Mississippi."

"Ok, I'll see you there."

CHAPTER THIRTEEN

Meanwhile in Virginia, Sarah was going insane without Max. The crazy thing about it, everybody knew she had lost it. However, she failed to accept it. Sarah had just begin to realize it! She missed her girls dearly. Sarah decided to go back to Saint Louis to spend time with her girls, old friends, and family members. "Perhaps I'll ignite some burnt out flames that ran away when I got saved. There shouldn't be any harm in that, mixing light with dark. I should be strong enough to go back and strengthen a brother or maybe two. Helping others always pulls me out of a slump." Sarah thought out loud.

The following day, Sarah purchased a one-way ticket from Virginia to Saint Louis. Lisa and her husband saw Sarah off at the airport. Sarah genuinely enjoyed herself with them, since they kept her laughing and her mind off of Max as much as possible.

She got some much needed rest on the plane while. The airplane landed in Saint Louis six hours later. Sarah's dad picked her up from the airport.

"Good to see you, sweetie! " Sarah's dad exclaimed. He gave Sarah a hug. Dang you big. You look like you about to have that baby now." He put the lounge in his truck. "When you due again?"

"In two weeks."

"More like two minutes."

They both laughed as the got into the truck.

Sarah resided at her mother's house with Hannah, and Haven. While out with friends, Sarah ran into her old fling, Ken. He wasted no time asking Sarah if he could treat her to lunch the next day. Sarah met Ken at the restaurant they always went to after a long morning of wake and shaking. They reminisced for a while. Sarah still thought he was the finest thing walking, which was until she met Max, of course. Since then, he had lost value.

After talking to him, she couldn't believe the change he had made throughout his life since the last time she had been with him. He stop selling drugs. He was no longer balling with the money the world had given him, but he was now balling with the money God allowed him to get. He got saved four years ago. He's now a preacher, and married with two kids. Back then, Sarah wouldn't have never seen it coming, not even with a microscope, but now that she knew Christ for herself, she knew He can and will save anybody if he wanted to be saved.

"You look pretty. How far along are you?"

"I'm due in less than two weeks."

"What are you having?"

"A boy." Sarah smiled.

"So I have a couple of questions for you," said Ken. He glanced at Sarah before looking down at his menu. "What made you accept my invitation to lunch? What brings you back to the Lou? Ken licked his lips. He felt them drying out due to the heat from his breath that penetrated them as he talked. *Did he just blow me a kiss*, Sarah thought to herself. She sat with curiosity. *Maybe I'm tripping? Well, I am looking kind of good today minus my enormous belly, he always said I was the best he ever had. Sarah entertained that thought a little while longer. Wait, he wouldn't do that.* "Devil I cast down those wicked thoughts you are trying to plant in my head," Sarah said under her breath. "You have no place here in my mind. I rebuke you in the name of Jesus,"

"Huh?" Ken said, breaking Sarah's train of thought.

Sarah took a sip of her ice cold water that was placed in front of her by their waiter. "Here you go with the questions."

"So which question are you going to answer Mrs. Smarty pants? I see you still haven't learned to tame that tongue of yours." He chuckled. "I'm not surprised, for no one can tame the tongue; it is a restless evil, full of deadly poison. Don't worry. Before we leave, we're going to pray that God set a guard over your mouth and keep watch over the door of your lips so that your tongue be gentle as a tree of life and not perverseness, for it breaks the spirit. We know when words are many, transgression is not lacking, but whoever restrains his lips is prudent." Ken smiled.

"Ay man, can you stop smiling at me, please. You're making me uncomfortable." Sarah turned her head and looked the other way. That was the same smile he uses to give her right before he caused her to go into voluntary confinement. Sarah broke into an instant sweat. "Oh, wee Jesus." She blurted.

"Oh, I'm sorry. I wasn't trying to make you uncomfortable." Ken put his napkin up to his mouth and pretended to wipe his mouth to hide his smile.

"To answer one of the three questions you asked me," Sarah said, gathering her composure. "I needed to get out, away from family and friends and away from all the noise. I wasn't looking to get anything out of this lunch date other than a good laugh and some good food because I know you are not cheap, and you don't mind breaking bread."

"Yeah, that's true, but can't nobody break bread like Jesus."

Sarah gave him a blank stare followed by a smirk, and she shook her head.

Ken laughed. "You will get that tomorrow. Does this have anything to do with your husband?"

"Somewhat."

"Your family and friends think you're crazy for leaving him? They think you should go back home?"

"Yes."

"But they don't understand that you're not only running from Max because of his lack of absence and somewhat strict behavior towards you. You're running away from yourself. You're trying to protect Max from you and the heartache you can bring upon him if you don't get control of the problems you're battling with within yourself."

"Sarah looked at him in shock.

"Sarah give me your hand. I want you to take a walk with me. Don't look so star struck. Your intuition of me is correct. Now take my hand."
Sarah placed her hand firmly on his.

"The thing you're battling with, God said you can't win this fight alone. You need your husband's help. The enemy has you thinking you need to isolate yourself to get rid of the problem, but this will only make it worse. Your husband is the only one that can help you through this. Don't be afraid to tell him what's going on with you. He will understand. Your secret will be safe with him. I see a brand new, big, two-story house with the initials M.S.H. on the front of it. It has a long driveway that wraps around to the entire house. In the backyard, there is a fence surrounding a large oval shaped built-in pool with a slide attached to it, and a furnished patio area set aside the pool. When you go into the house from the backyard, you step into a beautiful kitchen with peach and gray floor tile. There's an island that sits in the center of the floor with a built-in stove top. The kitchen has cabinets positioned up and down throughout it. The double wide refrigerator, conventional oven microwave, and dishwasher are stainless steel. There are eight bedrooms with walk in closets. The master bedroom has a fireplace separating the master bathroom and master bedroom. Each room is fully furnished, and that's not including the two-bedroom guest house attached to this house. There are nine bathrooms, one of which has a built-in sauna. On the back end of the house on the other side of the kitchen is a movie room. The movie room has a half of the dome in the shape of a circle hanging from the ceiling. That's where you will watch movies laying back in movie chairs that recline. The movie room has a built-in concession stand. Down the hall, I see the Initials A.H.H. This room has an indoor play area identical to Mc Donald's built in play center. There are several video games throughout this room like, motorcycle games, dance machine, basketball, foosball and a lot more. The house has an open concept. The living room has a skylight and one big bay window. I see you driving a Black truck, Range Rover. The seats have the initials B.D. on it. The license plates say 'baby doll'. God said all this will be yours, but you have to stay on the straight narrow path."

Sarah was quiet throughout the detailed description of her future home. It was overwhelming, but she knew that whatever God had for her, and her family was for them.

Ken let Sarah hand go and smiled. "Well, Sarah, it's been nice talking to you. I have to get going. I want an invite to your house warming when God blesses you with that house. Oh, and I want you to come pick me up in your new Range when you get it. Man, God has great things planned for you, Sarah. Don't allow the enemy to overthrow your faith and push you out of the will of God."

Sarah gave Ken a hug before they parted ways. She went to her mom's house and loved on her kids before they went to bed. She lay in the bed thinking about all the things Ken said to her earlier that day. She never described her dream house to him, yet he hit the nail on the head.

Sarah couldn't refrain from thinking about the ongoing mind blowing expedition she and Max had. Sarah sat up off the floor gazing out the beautiful, arched six-foot window of their newly built house onto her black, spotless Range Rover, Max just bought for her. She thought about how far they have come in their relationship the good and the bad.

"Are you okay?" asked Max rubbing Sarah on her back.

"No." She stood up to put on her clothes. Tears began to form in the wells of her eyes before running away as she did her current problem.

"I thought I could, but I can't. I thought I did, but I haven't forgiven you, for all the things you did to me."

Max jumped up off the floor in awe, putting on his clothes in hopes Sarah didn't run out of the front door and leave.

"Look," said Max staring into her eyes while holding both

of her hands. "I know I messed up. I can't change the past. I'm sorry, but I wouldn't want to because it helped me become who I am today-- all my failures, disappointments and disbeliefs. I have done better, and I am doing better, baby doll. The person you're upset with is no longer a part of me. I let him go when I grabbed a hold of Christ. I'm a changed man? Why can't you see that?" Max proclaimed.

In disbelief, Sarah tooted her nose and looked away from Max. The sound of his voice begging her to stay made her angry as it brought back memories of them that she buried long ago, in hopes to never live through again.

"If it's more time you need, I can give you that. I pray that you can find it in your heart to forgive me. I can't see myself with no one else, and I won't allow myself to. You can keep the house and the truck I bought you. I just ask one thing."

"What's that?" Sarah demanded, clearing her throat. She could feel the bandages from previous wounds Max gave her being pulled back, more so because she never allowed them to heal properly. A sense of regret, shame, resentment, and betrayal came over her while she awaited Max's response.

Max tugged her arm before bending down on one knee. He had tears in his eyes the size of hail stones. In his face lay hurt and disappointment. An enlarged frog sat in his throat and blocked his airway, making it impossible for him to breathe. He accumulated thirty pounds of fear that weighed his heart down. He overcame all those emotions in a split second and said, "Please don't divorce me!"

Sarah felt a kiss on her stomach then a warm touch on her face.

"Sarah."

Sarah tilted her head to escape the feeling of something crawling in her ear as she laid in bed.

"Sarah." The voice grew louder in her ear.

"Hmm." She opened her eyes slightly. She extended her arm and touched the blurry image in front of her. The warmed from her touch gave her chills and her stomach tossed.

"Sarah, Baby."

"Max is that you? What.."

"Yes, baby doll. It's me."

"What are you doing here?" She woke up completely.

"Baby I'm here to take you home."

Get Involved

Go to (Author SIC) Facebook page to join the conversation. Post your answers and view post from others.

Who's your favorite character and why?
What do you think Sarah is dealing with?
Have you ever been in a long distance relationship? How do/did you like it?
Do you think Sarah was crazy for not wanting Max to be there for the birth of their baby?
Do you think Sarah made a big mistake marrying Max? Would you have married Max?
Do you think Evans is jealous of Sarah? Why?
Was it wrong for Sarah to allow her mind to wander after meeting Mr. Censored?
Did you lead your mate now spouse to Christ? Explain.
Did this book help you in any way?
If you could change any part in this story, which part would it be? What would you have done different? Give a brief scenario.
Share your thoughts for a chance to have me turn them into a short story.
Want to take part in "The Ironworkers Wife" Part II? Tell me what you would love to happen.

Stay Connected
Facebook, Twitter: Author SIC
Instagram: Author_SIC
Email: author.sic@gmail.com
Website: www.authorsic.com

These are some scriptures that inspired me while writing this book.

PROVERBS 3:6
King James Bible
In all thy ways acknowledge him, and he shall direct thy paths.
God's Word translation
In all your ways acknowledge him, and he will make your paths smooth

EPHESIANS 3:20
King James Bible
Now unto him that is able to do exceeding abundantly above all that we ask or think, according to the power that worketh in us,
God's Word Translation
Glory belongs to God, whose power is at work in us. By this power he can do infinitely more than we can ask or imagine.
2 CORINTHIANS13:5
King James Bible
Examine yourselves, whether ye be in the faith; prove your own selves. Know ye not your own selves, how that Jesus Christ is in you, except ye be reprobates?
God's Word Translation
Examine yourselves to see whether you are still in the Christian faith. Test yourselves! Don't you recognize that you are people in whom Jesus Christ lives? Could it be that you're failing the test?
PHILIPPIANS 4:8
King James Bible
Finally, brethren, whatsoever things are true, whatsoever things are honest, whatsoever things are just, whatsoever things are pure, whatsoever things are lovely, whatsoever things are of good report, if there be any virtue, and if there be any praise, think on these things.
God's Word Translation
Finally, brothers and sisters, keep your thoughts on whatever is right or deserves praise: things that are true, honorable, fair, pure, acceptable, or commendable.

Galatians 5:26
King James Bible
Let us not be desirous of vain glory, provoking one another, envying one another.
God's Word Translation
We can't allow ourselves to act arrogantly and to provoke or envy each other.

Mark 11:26
King James Bible
But if ye do not forgive, neither will your Father which is in heaven forgive your trespasses.

Luke 4:13
King James Bible
And when the devil had ended all the temptation, he departed from him for a season.
God's Word Translation

After the devil had finished tempting Jesus in every possible way, the devil left him until another time.

1 Corinthians 7:2
King James Bible
Nevertheless, to avoid fornication, let every man have his own wife, and let every woman have her own husband.
God's Word Translation
But in order to avoid sexual sins, each man should have his own wife, and each woman should have her own husband.

Ecclesiastes 1:19
King James Bible
The thing that hath been, it is that which shall be; and that which is done is that which shall be done: and there is no new thing
under the sun.
God's Word Translation
Whatever has happened before will happen [again]. Whatever has been done before will be done [again]. There is nothing new under the sun.
Hebrews 10:25
King James Bible
Not forsaking the assembling of ourselves together, as the manner of some is; but exhorting one another: and so much the more, as ye see the day approaching.
God's Word Translation
We should not stop gathering together with other believers, as some of you are doing. Instead, we must continue to encourage each other even more as we see the day of the Lord coming.
Ecclesiastes 2:1
King James Bible
I said in mine heart, Go to now, I will prove thee with mirth, therefore enjoy pleasure: and, behold, this also is vanity.
God's Word Translation
I thought to myself, "Now I want to experiment with pleasure and enjoy myself." But even this was pointless.
Genesis 1:27
King James Bible
So God created man in his own image, in the image of God created he him; male and female created he them.
God's Word Translation
So God created humans in his image. In the image of God he created them. He created them male and female.
James 4:7
King James Bible
Submit yourselves therefore to God. Resist the devil, and he will flee from you.
God's Word Translation
So place yourselves under God's authority. Resist the devil, and he will run away from you.

John 14:26
King James Bible

But the Comforter, which is the Holy Spirit, whom the Father will send in my name, he shall teach you all things, and bring all things to your remembrance, whatsoever I have said unto you.
God's Word Translation
However, the helper, the Holy Spirit, whom the Father will send in my name, will teach you everything. He will remind you of everything that I have ever told you.

Galatians 5:7
King James Bible
Ye did run well; who did hinder you that ye should not obey the truth?
God's Word Translation
You were doing so well. Who stopped you from being influenced by the truth?

Romans 8:26
King James Bible
Likewise the Spirit also helpeth our infirmities: for we know not what we should pray for as we ought: but the Spirit itself maketh intercession for us with groanings which cannot be uttered.
God's Word Translation
At the same time the Spirit also helps us in our weakness, because we don't know how to pray for what we need. But the Spirit intercedes along with our groans that cannot be expressed in words.

2 Corinthians 5:17
King James Bible
Therefore if any man be in Christ, he is a new creature: old things are passed away; behold, all things are become new.
God's Word Translation
Whoever is a believer in Christ is a new creation. The old way of living has disappeared. A new way of living has come into existence.

Philippians 3:13
King James Bible
Brethren, I count not myself to have apprehended: but this one thing I do, forgetting those things which are behind, and reaching forth unto those things which are before,
God's Word Translation
Brothers and sisters, I can't consider myself a winner yet. This is what I do: I don't look back, I lengthen my stride, and

AUTHOR SIC

Starr I. Coburn was born and brought up in Saint Louis, Missouri. She migrated to Mississippi with her family, however travels frequently. She is a humble self-driven freelancer who is determined to provide her readers with story's that will inspire, uplift, challenge and recreate their way of thinking, in hopes that it will impact their life in an amazing way. She doesn't see failure as an option, so she strives to do better than she did before. She brings relatable experiences to life in her writing as she feeds off the world around her, this fuels her imagination. She believes that the same thing that makes you laugh can make you cry, hence in all of her life journeys she strives to discover the humor in it entirely.

Made in the USA
Charleston, SC
05 June 2016